D0469195

THE
TANGLEWOODS'
SECRET

THE TANGLEWOODS' SECRET

By Patricia M. St. John

MOODY PRESS
CHICAGO

First published 1948
by the Children's Special Service
Mission and the Scripture Union.
All rights reserved.

Moody Press Edition 1951

Twenty-ninth Printing, 1982
ISBN 0-8024-0007-8

Printed in the United States of America

Contents

Chapter 1

A SUGAR BUN FOR SUPPER

ONE EVENING when I was eight years old, I had been sent to bed without any supper and I was in disgrace. I lay in bed that beautiful evening listening for the stump, stump of a rather slow boy in football shoes, climbing the stairs to our attic.

When Philip, my brother, did come, it was straight to my room. He struggled with a queer-looking lump in his sock, then out came a squashed sugar bun. There was wool fluff stuck to the sugar and, yes sir, a woolly smell about it. Philip was proud of what he had done. It was right under Aunt Margaret's nose that he slipped it into his sock, and she never noticed! Oh, sure! I ate it, and Philip sat down on my bed to comfort me. I always liked plenty of sympathy at such times.

"What else did you have for supper?" I asked, with my mouth full of bun.

"I'm afraid we had sausages," he replied apologeti-

cally, "but they were too squashy to put down my sock.
They weren't very nice; you didn't miss much."

"It's very unkind of Aunt Margaret to send me to
bed without my supper," I started, in my most pathetic
voice. "If Mother were here, she wouldn't be unkind to
me like that."

"No," answered Philip, "she wouldn't. But then, you
see, you really were awfully rude to Aunt Margaret,
and you would never have been rude to Mother."

"How do you know?" I argued. "I might."

"Oh, no," he assured me, "you wouldn't. There
wouldn't be anything to be rude about. You're only
rude when you're cross, and we were never cross with
Mother. She was so happy and starry, and if we were a
little bit naughty she used to laugh, and pick us up in
her arms and tell us lovely stories, and we'd forget all
about being naughty. I wish you could remember her,
Ruth."

I opened my mouth to ask more, but Philip suddenly
hopped off my bed and dived, like a frightened rabbit,
across the hall. I heard a quick scuffle, then silence—
then the sound of Aunt Margaret's footsteps on the attic
stairs.

She went into Philip's room, and I heard her cross
over to him and tuck him in; I heard him say, "Goodnight, Auntie," in a rather breathless voice; then she

came across and stood in the doorway of my room. "Good night, Ruth," she said.

If I had answered and said I was sorry, she would have come over and tucked me in, too; but I hated saying sorry, so pretended to be asleep and gave a very loud snore, which deceived no one—least of all Aunt Margaret.

"I'm sorry that you are still in such a naughty temper," she remarked coldly, and turned away and went downstairs.

"Did she see that you weren't undressed?" I whispered loudly across the hall.

"No," answered Philip. "I pulled the bedclothes round my neck—good night, Ruth."

"Good night, Phil," I answered, and turned over toward the window and stared out into the darkness. My mind was full of what Philip had said about Mother. Mother would have come across and kissed me, whether I was sorry or not and then, of course, I should have been sorry, and we would have looked at the stars together. She would have told me stories. I fell asleep almost feeling her arms around me, but in my dreams she ran away from me. She and Philip went away together. When I tried to run after them my feet would not move.

Philip and I lived with our Aunt Margaret in a

beautiful home. It was a white house built on the side
of a hill. Oh, the beautiful sunsets we saw just behind
the hill; there was the garden, and the orchard full of
wonderful apple trees! We liked our bedrooms because
they were at the very top of the house. We left the
doors open so that we could shout or talk across. My
room and Philip's room each had a window. Sometimes
I thought I liked his the best because the view he had
was out on the garden and the pine trees on the hill;
mine looked out on the great plain with fields of
growing things and cherry trees which were gorgeous
when they were in blossom. Off in the distance was a
place where I had never visited. I wondered what it
was like over there, now wouldn't you? Sometimes my
view showed the green hills close to me; sometimes
they seemed misty and far away. I liked to think of the
hills as my fairyland where I would go visiting when I
grew up.

Philip used to come to my room in the morning and
we would listen to the early birds sing, or watch the sun
come up over my fairy field. We told each other stories
about what was going on away out there, and about the
animals we just knew must live among the trees in the
hills.

I loved my "big" brother Philip more than anyone
else. You see, he was one year and a half older than I, a

gentle boy, thoughtful, my friend, protector, and a comforter, too. We were always together except when at school.

Let me tell you how my brother, Philip, looked. He was sturdy, with a round face that always looked calm, and he had nice blue eyes. I was just the opposite, small, thin, with a sharp chin and with dark hair that never stayed where it should. Aunt Margaret loved Philip—who wouldn't? He was good and obedient. My aunt used to shake her head when she looked at me, because she said, "She takes years off my life." You know that was not so good, for it meant that if she had only Philip, and not me, she would live longer.

It is now the time of my story, so that means we had been with our Aunt Margaret five years. We had forgotten what Mother and Father looked like. I was only four years old when Mother and Father sailed away for the land of India to be missionaries. Mother was going to come back to us before too long, but there was a war and that stopped her from coming. Do you know, I think I really didn't want her to come back. You see, Aunt Margaret kept reminding me about how disappointed Mother would be in me. Her letters sounded as though she loved me very much, but then that was because she didn't know me, I thought.

Grown-up visitors always liked Philip, and I knew

Mother would, too. Philip would like Mother because he liked everybody. Me! I would much rather have and keep my brother Philip all to myself. On that account I thought of my mother coming back as seldom as I could. Philip talked about Mother because he remembered her, and I didn't.

Chapter 2

HOLIDAY PLANS

TWO YEARS after the night I told you about in the last chapter, I was nine-and-a half, and Philip was nearly eleven. On the first day of our Easter holidays, Philip came into my room in his pajamas at half-past six in the morning, and curled up on the end of my bed with his notebook and pencil in his hand; together we leaned our elbows on the window-sill to watch birds and to make plans.

Bird-watching was our great hobby that holiday. We had a notebook in which we recorded each different kind of bird we saw, and everything we noticed about it—its song, its nest, its habits. Philip had made the book himself, and it was beautifully neat and accurate. He did all the writing and I painted the eggs when we found them; but my drawings were not particularly good.

Philip longed for a camera with which to photograph his nests. "If only I could take photographs of them," he would say, over and over again, "I might be a great naturalist—my book might even be printed."

But the cheapest camera in the shop windows cost a great deal, and our money-box held about two dollars and fifty cents, even though we had been saving for weeks and weeks. We emptied the coins on to the quilt, and counted them over again, just in case we'd made a mistake the time before. But we hadn't. Philip sighed deeply.

"I shall nearly be going to boarding school by the time I get that camera," he said sadly. "I wish we could earn some money, Ruth."

We gazed out into the garden rather sadly, racking our brains for some plan; but nothing brilliant suggested itself to us. Below us, April had touched the fruit trees, and blossom foamed like a soft white sea over the plain. Our own damson plum trees were white and lacy, and I could see nests of primroses around their roots and golden daffodil trumpets resplendent in the sun. I looked across to my own hills, but they were hidden in the early haze of a spring morning. All of a sudden I felt Philip's body stiffen beside me, and he half dived out of the window in his eagerness.

"Tree creeper!" he hissed. "On the plum!"

I leaned out beside him and we watched together—a neat brown bird running up the tree, tapping the bark for insects; Philip was all alert now, noting every slightest pose and gesture—hardly drawing his breath until the little creature had spread his wings and disappeared round the corner. Then out came pen and notebook, and my brother was busy for five minutes.

"Ruth," he said eagerly, looking up at the end of that time, "we must get to the woods early today and have plenty of time—and Ruth, I was thinking in bed last night, we ought to have a naturalist's headquarters. We ought to build a place where we could keep pencils and rough paper and things in tins, instead of always carrying them with us—because we shall go every day all the holidays. And we must escape early before Aunt Margaret thinks of things we ought to do."

I nearly tumbled out of bed in my eagerness.

"We'll race through our holiday jobs," I announced, "and I'll be as good as gold, so she'll hardly notice me, and she won't watch me, and when I've swept and dusted in the drawing-room I'll just slip out before she thinks of anything else. If she asks where we've been we'll say we've been getting wood—and we'll bring a little back with us to make it true—but I don't see why we should have to work at all in our holidays! I know what I'll do—I'll dress quick, and go down now and help Aunt Margaret with breakfast to make her think how good I'm being!"

I was out of bed in a flash, and in ten minutes' time I duly presented myself in the back-kitchen, arrayed in a clean apron, with my hair in perfect order.

"Can I help you, Aunt Margaret?" I inquired meekly. "I got up early in case you might need me."

As I was noted for my lateness in the mornings, my aunt looked rather astonished.

"Thank you, Ruth," she answered pleasantly, hiding her amazement, "you can set up the table for me. I should be very glad."

Everything went smoothly. Philip and I bolted our breakfast and sat bottling up our impatience while Uncle Peter and Aunt Margaret sipped their second cups of coffee, discussing the day ahead. Then Uncle Peter went off, and Aunt Margaret turned to us.

"And what plans have you two made?" she asked.

Philip had the answer all ready. "As soon as we've done our holiday jobs, we're going to get wood, Aunt Margaret," he replied, in his sweetest voice.

"Very well," answered my aunt a little doubtfully, "but you must remember I need your help in the mornings; Ruth is old enough to assist in the house now; she shall start with wiping-up and doing the drawing-room, and then we'll see."

I could be quick when I liked, and I wiped up the breakfast things in an astonishingly short time. Then, without any further consultation with my aunt, I seized the broom and duster and made for the drawing-room. I poked the dust wildly round the linoleum with the broom, and flicked it off the ledges at top speed. I could not see the dust pan, but wasted no time about it—I gathered up my little heap and shoved it under the carpet. Then I tiptoed back to the kitchen, replaced the broom and duster, and was out of the front door like a streak of lightning.

Out and free on an April morning, with the sun shining, and the birds singing, and the lambs bleating! I tore round the back like a whirlwind and pounced upon Philip all unexpectedly, nearly knocking him over; but he was quite used to me by now, and was not much alarmed.

"Finished already?" he inquired, rather surprised.

"Yes; haven't you?"

"No," he answered. "I've got to chop these sticks into little bundles for kindling wood. It will take ages."

"Oh!" I cried. "We can't wait! You've made quite enough of those silly bundles. No one will know we haven't chopped them all up if they can't see the rest. Quick—give those sticks to me!"

And before my more conscientious brother could

protest, I had heaved the remainder into the ditch and was kicking the dead leaves over them.

"And think," I shouted, prancing up and down, "how quickly we shall find them when we are sent to get more!"—and with a final leap I was away across the orchard—away through the clean wet grass all starred with primroses, and out through the gap in the back hedge like a young rabbit, with Philip close at my heels.

The gap in the shrubbery was our own special right of way, and no one else knew about it. Aunt Margaret could see the gate from the kitchen window, and sometimes we preferred to keep our comings and goings to ourselves. So we had found a gap, behind the hen house, invisible to anyone else on account of the overhanging branches which we brushed aside. It led out into another meadow which led to the road, which in turn led to our woods.

Once in the road I danced and shouted like a young mad thing; it was sheer joy to be alive on such a morning. Philip followed more soberly, his eyes glued to the hedges, now and then stopping to listen or to watch. I did not wait for him; I felt as though spring had got into my feet; I think I scared away most of the birds before Philip came anywhere near them.

I vaulted the gate that led through the meadow, and

stood still for a minute watching the sober mother sheep with their merry long-legged lambs, leaping, like me, among the daisies. And as I watched, one of the lambs with a smudged nose and black stockings suddenly saw me and came rushing toward me, uttering little bleats of welcome; I squatted down and held out my arms; he ran straight into them, and started licking my face with his eager warm tongue.

"Philip!" I cried, "Philip, look what's happening!"

Philip was beside me by this time, and together we knelt in the grass while the little orphan prodded us, licked us, and leaped from one lap to another. As we played, an old shepherd came and leaned over the gate, smiling at us.

"That's the little orphan," he explained. "He's bottle fed, and he's not afraid of anyone. The other sheep push him away, so off he goes on his own. He's always in mischief, the wee rascal!"

The lamb at this moment leaped from my knee and ran to the gate; the old man stooped and picked it up.

"He knows my voice all right, doesn't he?" he remarked, smilingly. Then, tucking it inside his coat, he turned away toward the farm.

"That's a new shepherd," I said to Philip. "I've never seen him before."

"I have," answered Philip. "He's over for the lamb-
ing season. Come on, Ruth! We're wasting time."

He jumped up, and we raced across the open meadow with the wind blowing my braids out behind me;
then over a stile, and we were standing in our woods.

Chapter 3

THE WIGWAM

Now I am grown up, but I often shut my eyes when I am tired, and think about our woods in April with their tangle and their perfume and their flowers. Wood anemones on the ground, violets in the clearing, and the bluebell shoots pushing up everywhere. Sunshine fell through the oaks and lighted up the banks and hollows where frail wood sorrels were half buried in leaves, and squirrels and birds were busy everywhere. Philip and I left the path that day and fought our way through the young trees which seemed all bound together with honeysuckle. At last we paused to look around, and Philip took a seat on some moss while I squatted beside him.

"We'd better build our headquarters here," he announced. "It's a good home base for further excavations."

Philip liked long words, and sometimes read the newspaper in search of them, though he did not always understand them.

"How?" I inquired.

"Like a wigwam," explained Philip. "Look, can you see that little mountain ash tree just there? That will be our center prop. Now we'll collect branches, and lean them up against the middle, close together; then we'll bind them together with honeysuckle binding, and just leave a little doorway to creep through—and we'll have a floor of dead bracken and moss, very soft and comfortable—it will be almost like building a nest. Then at the back we'll dig a hole and line it with sticks and stones; we'll bury our supplies there, and cover them with bracken so you won't be able to see anything; it will look just like a floor."

I was thrilled, and set to work immediately; we worked hard all the morning, dragging dead boughs through the undergrowth and cutting long stakes with Philip's knife. Before long we had the skeleton wigwam firmly fixed, with a little doorway just large enough—though it was a tight squeeze for Philip.

It took us some days to complete our wigwam; every morning I rushed through my jobs and we made a bee-line for the woods. Every morning the pile of dust under the carpet grew bigger and bigger, but as Aunt

Margaret had done the spring-cleaning my laziness was not noticed.

Oh, those mornings in the woods! We didn't often keep together; we both wandered off on our own trail, happy with our own fancies, returning to the home base with armfuls of bracken and binding—each of us finding our own treasures and adventures and sharing them on our return.

Perhaps Philip's best find was the long-tailed tit's nest. I came across him crouching in a ditch, watching a hawthorn bush; he dragged me down beside him.

"Long-tailed tit," he breathed, "feeding young—she'll be back in a sec."

Even as he spoke there came a light whirr of tiny wings and the rustle of leaves, as the little mother flashed past with a morsel in her beak. We could hear the excited cheepings of the baby birds, and the general commotion that takes place in nests at mealtimes—then back she came on her anxious quest and disappeared into the wood.

"Now," whispered my brother, "let's look before she comes back!"

Cautiously we parted the boughs and stooped to look. There it was, a perfect little round ball of a nest, tightly woven with hair and grey lichen, with a door in the side. It seemed a miracle that such a tiny bird could have fashioned such a perfect home; and, as we watched, the nestlings became aware of our presence, and a crowd of agitated yellow beaks were thrust through the hole, accompanied by frantic chirpings. But we had no worms, and withdrew lest we should frighten the mother.

"She'll fledge them soon," said Philip, "and we'll hide in the ditch and watch."

We watched most of the time. We kept breaking away from what we were doing, and stealing back to visit our little neighbors; day by day as they grew and thrived and sprouted feathers their cries became stronger and more clamorous.

They were not our only neighbors; up in the beech tree above the wigwam was a high forked bough. One day, when I was quietly weaving the wall, I heard a rush of great wings—a brown owl swooped close past me. I was up the trunk in an instant, hoisting myself from branch to branch and searching every hollow and crevice for the nest. My search was rewarded, for there, in the topmost fork of the tree, cradled in straw and fluffy brown feathers, lay one pure white egg, hot from the mother's breast.

I climbed down a little way so as not to disturb the mother, and sat swinging my legs and looking about me. The slopes behind the woods were covered with bluebells. I was so happy that it almost hurt—and then I saw Philip, looking very small, moving slowly through the trees, his arms full of bracken.

"Phil!" I called. "Come up here!"

He was up in a minute; together we gazed in deep delight at the pure, precious thing. Then we caught sight of the mother sitting in the next beech, snapping her yellow eyes angrily, and we thought we had better go down; instantly she spread her great brown wings and dropped on to her nest; we slid down and discussed baby owls, lying on our tummies in the wigwam.

Everything went well for a week, and Aunt Margaret seemed content enough to let us go our own way. If ever I noticed her looking tired and over-worked, I told myself that it was not my business. My holidays were my own; I was going to spend them as I pleased, and in any case I wasn't much good at housework. So it was rather annoying when my aunt stopped me one morning, just as I was tearing out of the house, and asked me where I was going.

"Out with Philip," I answered, wriggling a little under her restraining hand. "I've done my jobs, honestly I have, Aunt Margaret. Please let me go; Phil's waiting for me."

"Well," replied my aunt quietly, "I think Philip must be content to go alone this morning. I need you,

Ruth. I've got a big wash this morning, and you can help me in hanging out the clothes and in other ways. It's time you did a lot more than you do."

I kicked the ground and looked just about as sullen as it's possible to look.

"But I specially wanted to go out today," I whined.

Aunt Margaret gave me a little shake.

"Well, you can just do what somebody else wants, for a change," she replied. "And if you can't do as you're told cheerfully, you can stay in this afternoon as well. You are getting more lazy and selfish every day; the sooner you take yourself in hand, the better."

She marched off to the kitchen and I followed, scuffling my feet and scowling. I was furious; why, the owl egg might hatch today, and I should miss it! The tits might come out of their nest, and Philip would see them alone. It wasn't fair! I hated Aunt Margaret at that moment, and I made up my mind I wasn't going to help her; I'd be as naughty as I could and then she'd be sorry she'd ever asked me to stay.

My thoughts were interrupted by the back door opening and Philip's head appearing. He had been working for Uncle Peter in the garden, and looked somewhat flushed and tousled.

"Coming, Ruth?" he asked, eagerly.

"No, she's not coming," replied my aunt shortly.

"She's going to make herself useful for a change. You run away and play by yourself this morning, Philip. Ruth can join you this afternoon, if she behaves."

We both had a miserable morning. I made ugly faces at the table and vented my wrath on things. I sighed and yawned and scuffled; I kicked the furniture, and scowled at my aunt's back; but she was working hard at the wash tub and pretended not to notice. She often pretended not to notice my tempers, and nothing annoyed me more; what was the good of being sulky when she would not even look at me? I grew crosser and crosser.

She noticed me all right in the end, however, because she told me to carry out a basin of clean handkerchiefs and hang them on the line. I did not really mean to do it, but I was so busy slamming the back door and rattling the clothes pins that the basin slipped from my hands, and all the handkerchiefs were scattered in the yard; it had rained in the night, too, and the yard was very muddy.

My aunt was very angry indeed. I think she would have liked to box my ears, for I saw her clasp her hands very tightly together; she told me the truth about myself in no uncertain terms; she said I might go now, as I was more trouble than I was worth on a busy morning. For a whole week I was to stay in every morning and work in the house. By the end of that time she hoped I would have learned how to be a little more pleasant and useful, and a little less clumsy. She spoke about my selfishness, and what a disappointment I should be to my mother; then she took the basin of muddy handkerchiefs out of my hands and went into the house.

I stamped my foot, gulped back my tears, and marched out of the gate with my head in the air. I had lost my mornings for a week, but there was an hour left before dinner—I would go to meet Philip, and walk home with him.

It was a very quiet morning, clouded and hazy and warm after rain; all the world smelled sweet and fresh and fragrant. Flowers lifted their heads again, birds sang with content, and I felt strangely out of place with my ugly, angry thoughts and my tear-stained face. I even stopped to think about it, and looked about me. There were the trees doing their work without haste or clamor, each leaf perfect in its unfolding, each opening bud a miracle; and there was no fret or needless hurry—just the peace of doing something well. I couldn't have put it into words then, but that peace seemed to enter into me for a few minutes. I stood thinking how perfect life could be if only I could be good.

I did not often want to be good, but I wanted it then—wanted with all my heart to be good, and happy, and useful—in harmony with God's world. I clasped my hands together and spoke aloud, because I wanted it so badly.

"I want to be good," I whispered. "I don't want to lose my temper and be selfish. Oh! Why can't I be good?"

But my words seemed to float away into the empty air, for I knew nothing of Him who stood so close to me, longing to help and change me. To me He was nothing more than a Person who had lived long ago, and about whom I had read and heard in church. So after a few minutes I shrugged my shoulders and went on.

"I never shall be," I muttered. "I shall always be horrid and cross, and nobody will ever like me."

I met Philip absolutely beside himself with joy; he did not seem to have missed me at all!

"I watched the egg hatch," he announced. "I went up and she flew off; when I looked, the shell was cracked and I could see that thin skin heaving up and down; I daren't stay in case it got cold and the owlet died. She's back now, brooding on it, and I shouldn't go up if I were you, because she might peck you."

There wasn't time to go up, in any case, as it was high time to go home to dinner. On the way I told Philip of my tragic morning. He was comforting and sympathetic, and I felt better, even though knowing perfectly well that I deserved no sympathy. Then, in his own thoughtful way, he stopped talking about the mornings and we spent the rest of our walk home planning the afternoons.

Chapter 4

TERRY

THREE DAYS LATER we had our first adventure and
made a new friend; and this is how it happened.
The wigwam was well and truly finished and as snug
a little house as anyone could wish, with its secret
hiding-place where we hid our tea and other belongings
when we went exploring. The tits had left the nest, we
had watched their first uncertain flight, and had seen
them flounder on to the moss, screaming for their
mother. The owlet, too, was growing; he now resem-
bled a ball of soft grey cotton wool, with a hooked beak
and round yellow eyes. He seemed to have no objection
to our holding him in our hands. We had found other
nests, too: blackbirds', thrushes', and hedge-sparrows'
in the bushes, and a starling's in a hollow willow trunk;
these we visited every day, writing daily reports on
their progress.

That afternoon about which I am going to tell was

bright and windy; the wind was behind us, blowing
strongly from the hills. We had been caught up in it
and had run all the way. Being carried along made us
laugh, and we reached the wigwam quite breathless
with running and laughter, ready to fling ourselves
down on the mossy floor and recover our breath in the
cool, dark shade of its walls. So it was quite a shock to
me when Philip, who had dived half-way through the
entrance, suddenly backed out, his eyes wide with astonishment, and whispered dramatically,

"The wigwam is occupied!"

"Who by?" I inquired indignantly, backing a step or
two.

"Well, I couldn't exactly see," replied Philip, "but I
think it's a boy."

"Well," I said loudly, "it's our wigwam, and he'd
better come out, because we want to go in."

There was a dead silence.

"You'd better come out!" said Philip, very loudly
and clearly.

Still no answer.

"Perhaps it's a dead body?" I suggested.

"No, it isn't," answered Philip. "I saw it scratch
itself."

There was a long, uncertain silence; Philip began to
giggle.

"I think I'd better go in and look again," he said. "Perhaps he's deaf."

He went down on hands and knees and approached the entrance with extreme caution; his front half disappeared into the doorway, and another long silence ensued.

"Hurry up!" I exclaimed impatiently, taking hold of his legs in my excitement. "Who is he? And what is he doing?"

"We're just staring," said Philip with another giggle. "It's a boy, as I said—I say, boy, this is *our* wigwam, and we're coming in, so you'd better get out."

"Shan't!" said a voice from within.

"Then I shall pull you out," said Philip, with perfect good humor.

"Then I shall catch hold o' the wall and pull it down with me," answered the voice coolly.

Another silence, while the rivals eyed each other narrowly, and I danced up and down with excitement and indignation.

Philip broke the silence.

"I know," he said, "let's have a tournament, like in the history book!"

"A how much?" inquired the voice; its owner seemed unfamiliar with history books.

"A tournament," repeated Philip. "It's like a fight

between two people who are having a quarrel. Whoever wins the fight wins the quarrel. You come out and fight, and if I win you go away, but if you win you can share the hut. Because, after all, you know, we *did* build it."

Our uninvited visitor seemed to like this idea, for I saw Philip wriggle out of the entrance backwards and roll merrily over on to the ground, thus making room for him to come out. And, angry as I was, the minute I saw his face I liked him and wanted to know him.

"I hope Philip wins," I thought to myself. "But all the same, I hope he'll stay and play. I like him."

He was a little boy, about as big as I, but the same age as Philip. His clothes were ragged and rather too small for him, but his eyes were as bright as a blackbird's, and his thin face was as brown as a berry and freckled. His thick hair fell down over his forehead; in his arms he held an enormous bunch of flowers—kingcups and cowslips. He laid them carefully on the moss and bade me "let 'em alone while he knocked out that toff."

The "tournament" began in a highly irregular fashion, before anyone was ready for it, for the boy suddenly ran at Philip and punched him on the jaw. Philip, taken by surprise, had not the time to hit back before he was punched again on the ear; and even then he stood and blinked several times before making up his mind what to do about it.

"Hit him, Phil!" I yelled, nearly joining in myself, and beating the nearest tree to relieve my feelings.

It was a good fight to watch, once Philip got fairly started; Philip was as strong and as determined as an ox, but the boy reminded me of a little ferret. He twisted and turned, and leaped and wriggled, his thin brown arms bulging with muscle, and his lips pressed tightly together. Back and back he came, while Philip stood his ground and measured out slow, relentless blows. It was a very exciting fight indeed, and I behaved like a whole gallery of spectators rolled into one.

The boy won; he pretended to spring at Philip's neck, and then suddenly changed his tactics, and dived between his feet, bringing him to the ground with an alarming crash. By the time Philip had realized what was happening, the boy was sitting on his chest, thumping him with all his might.

"Stop it!" said Philip, coolly; "you've won."

"Beat yer 'ollow!" said the boy, getting up. "But I don't want yer silly ol' hut. I could build a better one meself."

He was gathering up his flowers and making off, when Philip ran over to him and held him by the suspenders he was wearing.

"Don't go!" he said "We'd quite like you to share the hut, and then perhaps one day we'll have another fight. I love fighting, don't you?"

"Not bad," said the boy.

"We're going to have tea now," urged Philip. "Come and have it with us. There's room for all three inside."

It was not nearly tea-time really, but we both felt we must do something to hang on to the boy—and at the word "tea," a remarkable change came over him. He stopped looking sullen and bored, and suddenly became interested. Without even troubling to say "Yes," he squatted down on the moss with an expectant smile on his face, and held out his grubby hand; when he smiled, and the light came into his eyes, I thought he looked quite handsome.

He must have been terribly hungry, for I have never seen anyone eat at such a speed either before or since! We opened our packet of sandwiches, and without so much as a Please or Thank-you he fell upon them and finished three while Philip and I were still eating our first; although our appetites were fairly healthy, too! Then, when the last crumb had disappeared and he had licked the jam off the paper, he gave a sigh of relief and we settled down to get to know each other.

We lay on our tummies, our faces cupped in our

hands, and the bluebells tickling our chins. The after-noon sun came slanting through the trees in golden bars and made leaf-shadow patterns on the ground; up above, the wind sighed and mourned in the treetops; but we were sheltered and warm and peaceful.

"What's your name?" asked Philip.

"Terry," he replied, and went on chewing a piece of grass.

"How old are you?"

"Eleven in August."

"Where do you live?"

"At the cottage in the 'ollow by the stream, down Tanglewoods way."

"Have you any brothers and sisters?"

"No—there's only me and Mum."

"Where's your father?"

" 'Aven't got none."

"What are all those flowers for?"

"Me Mum sells 'em in the town—she's a flower-seller."

"Do you pick them all for her?"

"Yes, when I can cut school."

Nobody spoke for a time; then I suddenly had an idea. I put my hand on his arm.

"Would you like to see an owl's nest?" I asked.

For answer he pointed upward to the tree. "That

one?" he asked. "I've seen 'im once today; got a little tame one from that nest last year; it stopped with me almost on two months."

I felt a little bit annoyed; it was *our* owl's nest, and he had no business to get there first; but Philip was before me. He leaned eagerly over toward the boy.

"Do you know lots of nests?" he asked. "Could you show us any more?"

He looked at us rather scornfully.

"I could show yer almost every nest in this 'ere wood," he replied.

Philip jumped to his feet. "Come on!" he cried. "Let's go and see! Show us them all, Terry!"

Terry got up slowly and looked us up and down, as though making up his mind as to whether we were the sort of children to be trusted with nests. Then he nodded.

"Right!" he answered briefly, and dived into the bushes.

A breathless hour followed. At the end I was quite exhausted and nearly torn to pieces, for Terry never stopped at an obstacle. We waded knee-deep in a pond to inspect a reed-warbler's woven home, and we swarmed impossible trees in search of crows' nests. We inspected holes in trunks, and watched a starling fly in and out. The wood was opened up to us, and we found out more about it in that hour than ever before. The sun was setting when we turned home.

"Good-by," we said, and we hesitated. Must this be the end? Would such a wonderful boy want to see us again?

"Coming again?" said Terry casually, and we heaved a great sigh of relief. From that moment Terry was our friend. Better still, we knew that he looked upon us as his friends.

Chapter 5

THE LOST LAMB

WE SAW TERRY nearly every day, and the time passed only too quickly; he led us all over the countryside and showed us his secret nests and lairs and burrows; we learned to identify and track the footprints of little animals, and to recognize the different cries of birds and what they meant. He dragged us through swamps and marshes and brambles in search of the earliest flowers, and showed us where to gather rare orchids. It was as though he had opened up to us a new world of wonder. We both loved and admired him for his amazing knowledge of woodland life. Before, I had always disliked Philip's friends, because I thought they took him away from me, but Terry seemed to think us both equally his friends. He never looked down on me for being a girl, and younger.

So it was a disappointment to us all when Philip

twisted his ankle while swinging from a tree, and, after
hobbling home, had to lie upon a couch for three days.

I stayed at home at first to help amuse Philip; I
believe my efforts were quite successful, but they nearly
drove Aunt Margaret to distraction. I started by
catching a duck and bringing it in, dressed up in a
doll's bonnet, to call on the invalid, and then letting it
loose on the dining-room carpet. We forgot it after a
little while; it waddled out into the hall, where it met
my aunt, who was *not* pleased to see it. We heard it
being shown out of the front door in a great hurry,
squawking angrily, after which we watched it waddling
across the lawn, the pink silk bonnet turning from side
to side as the duck looked about.

That diversion having been stopped, we decided to
play soldiers, and settled ourselves one at each end of
the dining room with a lead army and a dozen marbles
each. We bombed each other quite happily for a time,
till it suddenly struck us that the kittens in the wood-
shed would make excellent army cavalry. Off I trotted,
returning with an armful of soft, purring, black and
tabby fur, which I dropped on the floor. Four blue-eyed
kittens with twitching tails and whiskers sorted themselves out and rushed into corners.

I selected a tabby and a black-and-white, and Philip
had two coal-blacks to represent his army. We let fire

on the leaden infantry, and then the cavalry charge began.

It was a marvelous game, and the kittens loved it; they tore after the marbles in all directions, slaughtering the soldiers right and left. Philip and I shrieked with laughter and crawled round on all fours collecting our ammunition and recapturing the cavalry. Faster and faster ran the kittens, fiercer and fiercer grew the battle, when suddenly there was a crash and a splash. Tabby had leaped on to a dangling tablecloth and pulled it, together with a vase of flowers, over on top of himself. Of course, at that moment the door opened and Aunt Margaret came in.

The kittens instantly rushed between her feet; one stopped and dug his tiny claws into her stocking. The wicked tabby, unable to disentangle himself, rolled over and over all wrapped up in the tablecloth. The flower water streamed across the carpet, and Philip and I lay flat on the floor and laughed until the tears ran down our cheeks.

My aunt was not amused. I will not describe the scene that followed, but it finished up with four very excited little kittens being banished to the cellar, and one very cross little girl being turned out of the house. Philip was given a book, and put back on the sofa.

I spent the next ten minutes or so sitting on the

woodpile sulking; it wasn't fair! Aunt Margaret had said it was all my fault, and it had been Philip's fault just as much as mine that time, so I told myself. I had actually suggested the kittens, but Philip had thought it an awfully good idea, and, anyhow, why shouldn't we play together? I didn't like being sent off alone like that. I hated Aunt Margaret—and, when you come to think of it, it wasn't me at all, it was the kitten. At that point I suddenly thought of that wet tabby rolling round inside the tablecloth; I began to giggle, and felt better.

I got up and went over to smell some early lilies of the valley that were coming out under the wall; by this time I was quite happy again. After all, it was very nice to be out of doors on a sunny spring day, even if I was alone. I decided to go to the woods and see if I could find Terry anywhere, so I squeezed through the gap and strolled down the road.

Spring was thinking about giving place to early summer; the lamb field was yellow with buttercups, and most of the lambs looked quite middle-aged. All around me I could hear their high, thin cries, and the deep answers of their mothers. I stopped and made a daisy chain, and wondered what had happened to the tame, motherless lamb who had sucked my fingers on the first day of the holidays.

I didn't go far into the wood, for the sun was pleasant on the outskirts and I wanted to pick flowers. The fern was already beginning to shoot up and hide the bluebells, and orchids and woodruff grew in the clearings. I wandered round, dreaming of Philip and Terry, and Mother, and nests, and the far-away hills, and bluebells, and wigwams, until I had almost forgotten where I was. It gave me quite a surprise to hear a man's voice quite close to me.

I looked up quickly, but he was not calling me; he was standing with his back to me, peering into the thickets; he had not seen me at all. But I recognized him at once; it was the shepherd who had picked up the orphan lamb and carried it under his coat.

Being rather inquisitive, I wanted to know what he was doing, so I went and stood where he could see me. As soon as he caught sight of me, he smiled broadly.

"Why!" he exclaimed. "You're the little maid who played with the lamb t'other day—and here you are a-turning up again just at the right moment. One of the little rascals 'as strayed, and I'm thinking as how he's caught somewhere here in these bushes, but I can't just see where. Maybe you'll stop and help find him."

I was only too delighted. Here was something nice to do, and a pleasant companion to do it with, so I set to work with great good will. I liked this old man with his white hair and his rosy face, and I felt he liked me; we were soon talking away as though we had known each other all our lives.

"Why did he stray?" I asked, as we parted the bushes and searched the ditches.

"Well," answered the old man, with a smile, "I reckon he's just like the rest of us; he likes his own way, and his own way's led him into trouble, poor little chap!"

"Well," I remarked, "I expect he's sorry for it now—all tied up in the bushes, and wishing he'd stayed in his meadow."

"Aye," agreed the old man, thoughtfully. "It takes a deal of thorns and briers to teach them lambs as their own way isn't the best one—he'll be crying his heart out for me now, maybe, if only I could find the place."

"Won't he be glad to see us!" I observed. "Oh! I'm longing to find him! I expect he'll be awfully tired and hungry. Have you anything for him to eat?"

He put his hand into his pocket, and drew out a bottle.

"You'll see!" he said. "The minute I pick him up in my arms, he'll have his nose in my pocket. He knows I wouldn't forget 'im—the little sinner!"

He chuckled softly, and we moved farther into the wood.

"He's strayed a long way, hasn't he?" I remarked.

"True," answered the old man, "but I'll find him yet. I've never yet had a lamb go astray, but what I've found him and brought him home; I always hear them crying out somewhere or other, although at times 'tis a long search."

"What's the longest you've ever searched for?" I asked.

" 'Most one night," he replied, "but that was in a storm, and I could scarce hear her cryings for the wind and the thunder. She was caught fast in a bramble bush, and I found her at dawn by lantern light—well-nigh dead with cold and hunger and crying."

"And what did you do?" I asked again.

"Do?" repeated the old man. "Why, I set her free and quietened her, and wrapped her in my coat, and carried her home; she was like a mad thing when we found her, but once she felt my arms round her she lay as quiet as a baby—she knew there was nothing more to be a-feared of then!"

I was about to ask another question, but he suddenly held up his hand and stood perfectly still, listening.

I had heard nothing, but his practiced shepherd's ear had caught the sound at once—the faint cry of a tired lamb calling for help.

"That'll be him," he said simply, "in those bushes." And he made straight for the sound.

It was a wonder to me, when we saw him, how the little creature had ever got in. The hedge was so matted and the briers so thick; and it was a still greater wonder to me that the shepherd ever got him out. But we started parting the boughs, and as he worked he spoke to the lamb as a mother might speak to a frightened little child.

I don't suppose the lamb understood the words, but he knew the voice in an instant—knew in a flash that he was sought and found and loved, and at the sound of it ceased his weak struggles and fretful crying; he gave one joyful bleat and then lay still and waited.

It took a long time to reach him. I stood and watched while the old man patiently worked at the tangle, thorn by thorn, and brier by brier; when he finally picked up the little prodigal his hands were dreadfully scratched and bleeding, but he didn't seem to notice; he just held that trembling lamb close and let it nuzzle its black nose trustfully into his pocket.

"Are ye ready to come home?" he whispered, playfully lifting the little smudged face to his own.

"Baaa!" said the lamb, and put its nose back into the shepherd's pocket.

We walked home quietly, my small hand clasped in

the shepherd's large horny one, and the lamb lying in the crook of his arm. He seemed to be thinking deeply and his face looked very happy. I longed to share his thoughts, but did not like to ask, so I said nothing.

When we reached the field, the sun was setting and the sky behind the bluebell slopes was the color of pink shells. We laid the lamb among the others, and he gave a bleat of content and fell fast asleep.

"Well," I said slowly, "I suppose I'd better be getting home now; thank you for letting me help, and I hope I'll see you again soon."

But he drew me down beside him on the wooden bench that ran round the outside of the fold. "Before you go, little maid," he said, "I'll read you a bit of a story about another sheep as strayed." And as he spoke, he took a small, worn New Testament from his pocket, and opened it at Luke, chapter fifteen; then he began to read, in his slow, kind, country voice.

I suppose I had heard the story before, but it had never interested me. But then it was different; it seemed to belong to the sloping buttercup fields, and the long evening shadows and the pink sky, and the sleeping folded sheep. I rested my head against the shepherd's shoulders and listened with all my heart.

"And when he hath found it, he layeth it on his shoulders, rejoicing.

"And when he cometh home, he calleth together his friends and neighbors, saying unto them, Rejoice with me; for I have found my sheep which was lost.

"I say unto you, that likewise joy shall be in heaven over one sinner that repenteth."

He closed his Testament, and I looked up at him.

"Good night, little maid," he said.

"Good night," I answered, "and thank you very much." And I walked slowly home through the buttercups.

Chapter 6

A BRILLIANT IDEA

I NEVER TOLD PHILIP about the shepherd—at least, not about the last bit—because I was afraid he would laugh and think it queer, and I should not have liked that. I almost forgot about it next day, because I had one of my brain-waves, and when I had a brain-wave I could never think of anything else until I had carried it out.

It came about next day, when Philip was hobbling round the garden, not yet being able to walk to the woods. We had played all our usual games, and were lying under the apple trees wondering what to do next. As there wasn't anything much to do, we just lay and chatted, and Philip started talking about his book again.

"It's getting very fat, Ruth," he assured me, "and it's full of useful information about birds. All I'm waiting

for now is the camera to take the pictures—and I shan't
get it for years. Just think," he went on dreamily,
"what a beautiful picture that baby owl would have
made when he sat on our hands!—and those tits sitting
in a row on the hawthorn bush."

"Never mind," I said comfortingly, "we've got more
than when we last counted, so we're getting on!"

"But it's so slow," sighed Philip. "I shall soon be
nearly grown up, and I expect I shall be sent to
boarding school, and there won't be much chance to
take pictures. I wish Auntie would let me be an errand
boy, and earn something in my spare time."

I interrupted his thoughts by suddenly pouncing on
him and slapping him violently on the back.

"Philip!" I shouted, "I've had a most marvelous
idea!"

"What is it?" he asked, doubtfully; he was a little
suspicious of my good ideas—they so often turned out
badly and ended up with punishments.

"It really is a good idea this time, Philip," I urged,
"and Aunt Margaret could never discover. We'll pick
flowers, like Terry's mother does, and sell them; we'll
earn money. Do say 'Yes,' Phil! It would be such fun!"

Philip was still extremely doubtful.

"But Terry's mother wouldn't like it," he objected,
"because if they bought our flowers, they wouldn't buy

hers as well, and then she wouldn't get so much money."

"Oh, we shan't go to the same places," I assured him. "She sells hers in the street in the town; we'll go to people's back doors—and we'll dress up a bit to look like gypsies."

Philip's eyes danced; he was coming round fast, as I knew he would sooner or later.

"Let's go to the big houses halfway up the hill, where they have big iron gates and drives," he said. "We'll dress up in our oldest clothes like gypsy children, and we'll make our faces a bit dirty and wear our muddiest shoes; you tie your braids up in your red hanky, and we'll get money. Let's start soon!"

I always liked to carry out all my plans instantly, and leaped to my feet immediately. Then I remembered Philip's ankle, and tried to curb my impatience.

"You'll be able to walk tomorrow, won't you?" I pleaded. "Although, even if you couldn't, a little limp would be quite helpful. It would make people sorry for you. We could say, 'Pity the poor lame beggar!' and hold out a hat, and you could put a big white hanky round your ankle and look as though it hurt you; only you wouldn't have to do it too much, because it would make me laugh."

I laughed at the very thought, and rolled about joyfully in the grass.

Philip's ankle was much better next day, and we escaped early and made for the woods with a big wicker shopping-basket. We were going to pick all the morning and sell all the afternoon; we had no idea of prices, which rather worried us, but we were trusting to luck rather than to judgment, and hoped for the best.

"Where are you going?" I asked Philip, as we reached the stile.

"Down to the swamp in the hollow," he replied. "I'm going to pick lots of cowslips, and there are some late kingcups out. I might find some orchids, too, to put in with the cowslips; the colors go well together."

"We can get some wild cherry blossoms, too," I added, "and I'm going to pick little bunches of wood sorrel and violets for tiny pots. We'll sell them cheap to the people who don't want big bunches. Oh, Phil! What fun it will be!"

I was dancing down the sloping path that led to the swamp, and nearly collided with a swinging bough of cherry blossom swaying low across the path. I stopped to pick some, and Philip caught up with me. He did not help me, but stood quietly staring up at the pure clusters.

"Isn't it beautiful?" he remarked slowly. "It's like great snowdrifts up there."

"Yes," I answered absently. "Pick some, Philip! I'm doing all the work."

"Isn't it a pity," went on Philip, taking no notice of me, "that it doesn't last? It will all have fallen in a few days, and the blossom will be all brown and ugly. Nothing beautiful really lasts, does it?"

"Oh, there'll be some bird cherries later on, I expect," I answered, in a matter-of-fact voice. "Stop staring, Philip! It's silly to think about things like that; pick some flowers."

Philip stooped down and started gathering large late violets, but his blue eyes were sober. I marched on rather crossly, for I didn't like Philip in these melancholy moods. But although I tried to forget them, his last words kept ringing in my ears: "Nothing beautiful really lasts, does it?"

It was quite true. All the nasty things like tempers and rows with Aunt Margaret went on and on, and you couldn't get rid of them; they might stop for a time, but you knew they would always come back; while beautiful things like holidays, and blossom, and sunsets, and birds singing, faded and died, and left you empty. Certainly other beautiful things came and took their places, but it didn't comfort you for the ones that had gone.

"Not one single thing," I said aloud to Philip.

"Not one single what?" inquired my brother; he had seen a jay, and had forgotten all about everything else.

"Beautiful things lasting," I explained, rather vaguely.

"Oh!" said Philip. "No, I suppose not, but it doesn't really matter, because more come. Jays usually nest low down, so keep your eyes open."

As he had not yet told me about the jay, I could not see what that had to do with it, but I was quite used to my brother's one-track mind, and said no more. In any case, we had nearly reached the swamp, so we turned our serious attention to the flowers.

We picked hard all the morning, and quite filled the shopping-basket with our bunches. There were golden balls of cowslips mixed with vivid purple orchids and lacy white woodruff. The dazzling brightness of the buttercups we veiled with cow parsley, and mingled the kingcups with cotton grass. The blossom we left by itself, for we felt that its perfect whiteness was best unadorned. I carried it separately, while Philip carried the basket. We hid all our flowers in the orchard, and went in to dinner, inwardly bubbling over with excitement, but outwardly quite calm.

Aunt Margaret looked rather hard at Philip, who was gobbling his dinner at a tremendous pace. She was a little suspicious of our haste to be off again.

"Philip," she asked rather severely, "I think you should rest that foot this afternoon. You've done enough walking on it this morning."

Philip turned injured blue eyes upon her.

"Why, Auntie," he assured her, in his most polite voice, "I've been standing still nearly all the morning. I just went to the bog and stayed there and picked a few flowers. I think, too," he added seriously, "that a lot of exercise makes it feel better. It stops it getting stiff. In fact, I had planned to walk on it as much as possible this afternoon."

And Philip, as usual, had his way, as he always did with my aunt.

"Very well," she agreed, "but don't overdo it—and keep out of that bog; your sister's shoes are a perfect disgrace."

Philip looked at my shoes and sighed. He, of course, had remembered to change his before Aunt Margaret noticed them; I, of course, had not. How calm life would be, I thought rather bitterly, if I had been born like Philip!

Aunt Margaret went into the kitchen to wash up after dinner. She did not ask me to help her, and I certainly did not offer. I was always full of excuses and arguments when asked to help, and my aunt was rather tired today, so she let it be.

Once the door was firmly closed, I fled upstairs. I untwisted my braids and my hair fell dark and loose to my waist. Then I tied up my head in my Indian hand-kerchief that Mother had sent me, and put on a dirty pinafore. My muddy shoes needed no touching up. I looked a perfect little vagabond. Philip in his bird's-nesting coat and boots looked a fit companion for me.

"Don't let Aunt Margaret see us," he whispered cautiously, as we slipped out of the door. "She'd have fifty fits! We'd better go through the gap."

We climbed the hills that led to the big houses rather slowly, for the day was hot and the basket was heavy; also Philip's ankle hurt quite a bit, although he would not admit it. What really worried us was the fact that the flowers were drooping so. Of course, we should have put them in water overnight, but we had been too impatient to wait till next day. Yet, in spite of our impatience, when we actually reached the first pair of iron double gates we seemed in no hurry to go in.

"What are you going to say?" asked Philip, rather nervously.

"Me?" I replied indignantly. "I'm not going to say

anything. You've got to say it; you're much better at all that sort of thing than me."

"Oh, well," said Philip peaceably, "perhaps we shan't have to say anything. Perhaps the person who lives here will come to the door and say, 'What beautiful bunches of flowers! I'll buy two'—and then we shall just smile and hand them over, and she'll give us some money and we'll go away."

This charming prospect cheered us up a lot, and we walked quicker until the path divided; the left-hand path ran round the front between beautiful lawns, flower-beds and cedar trees; the right-hand one ran round to the back.

"Do we go front or back?" I asked.

"Back, I think," said Philip. "After all, we mustn't forget we're gypsies."

Our timid knock at the back door sounded dreadfully loud—so loud that we both jumped. We had hardly had time to recover ourselves before the door was flung open and a housemaid appeared. She was a very grand housemaid with dyed hair and a permanent wave, and there was a heavy smell of perfume about her.

"Well?" she asked, sharply.

It all happened so suddenly that we were both quite taken aback, and simply looked at each other. There was a moment's silence, then a violent desire to scream

with laughter seized me. I could *not* speak. I turned
away from Philip with shaking shoulders, but not before I had seen that he was feeling as bad as I was. He
whisked out his handkerchief and pretended to sneeze
into it, but the result was a sort of cross between a snore
and a roar, which set me off worse than ever. The tears
streamed down my cheeks and I turned my back on the
housemaid.

"Well?" she asked again. This time she sounded
downright angry, so Philip controlled himself and answered in a very shaky voice.

"Would you like to buy some flowers?" he asked in
trembling voice.

"Good gracious, no!" replied the girl. "What in the
world should we be buying flowers for here? Didn't you
see the gardens? The mistress has more flowers than
she knows what to do with. Besides, those what you've
got in the basket are all dead."

"Oh, they'll be all right in water . . ." I began, but
she had already slammed the door in our faces, and we
were left giggling feebly on the steps.

I wiped my eyes on my pinafore, because I had
forgotten my handkerchief, and we made off down the
drive between beautiful beds of lilies of the valley and
wallflowers which we had been too excited to notice
when we came. We kept relapsing into peals of laugh-

ter, and were too amused to feel disappointed. Anyhow, we were certain we should be more fortunate next door. After all, the girl had been rather funny; her lips were so scarlet, and her nose was so big.

The next house certainly looked less grand; the garden was smaller, and we could see the front door from the road. We stopped a minute to read the notice on the gate. It said "NO PEDDLERS, NO CIRCULARS," in large capital letters.

"What does that mean?" I asked.

"I don't know," answered Philip. "Anyhow, it couldn't mean us, so come on!"

We walked up the path, holding the basket between us. "Whatever happens, we mustn't laugh this time," said Philip. "Don't let's look at each other at all; let's just both talk fast, and we shall be all right. And let's go to the front door, because perhaps the masters and mistresses will be nicer than the maids."

We climbed a flight of stone steps, and I pulled the bell handle rather harder than I meant to. It rang so loudly that Philip put his hands over his ears and went quite pale; it seemed awful to have made such a noise on such a quiet afternoon. We gave each other a desperate look, and at that moment the door opened; an elderly lady with an eye-glass and a very straight back opened the door and stood looking down at us as though she didn't like us much.

We were so determined to have no awkward pauses this time that we both started talking at once, very fast and loud:

"We've picked some flowers," said Philip.

"And we thought you might like to buy them," said I.

"They are about ten cents, I think," said Philip.

"Unless you think it's too much," said I.

"They look a bit dead," added Philip.

"But they'll be quite all right when you put them in water," said I.

"Because they are really quite fresh," said Philip.

"We only picked them today," said I.

During this surprising flood of conversation, the old lady stood staring at us in indignant astonishment. She took no notice of the withered bunch of cowslips that I was feverishly trying to push into her hand, and asked in an icy voice:

"Little boy and girl, did you not read the notice on the gate?"

"Yes," admitted Philip, rather puzzled.

"I'm sure I'm not a circular," I chimed in, rather pertly.

"Little boy and girl," went on the old lady in an

awful voice, "if you are too young to understand the English language, you are certainly too young to be doing this sort of thing. Go home to your mother!"

And for the second time that day we found ourselves standing on the steps with the door shut in our faces.

Philip was discouraged, and suggested going home; but I was more persevering, and urged him on.

"Let's try again!" I pleaded. "They can't all be as nasty. Look, this next gate says nothing about circulars, so it must be all right."

"Neither did the first one," murmured Philip, but he followed obediently inside, and we set off up the drive, the basket growing heavier and the day growing hotter every minute.

There was a beautiful rock garden on one side of the path. I was walking a little ahead when I suddenly noticed a clump of brilliant bell gentians nestling in a crevice; never before had I seen such a heavenly blue, and in an instant I had squatted down on the path to examine them more closely. At the same moment, Philip, trudging along behind me, saw a skylark soar upwards and remain poised and motionless. He threw his head back and walked on, forgetful of everything else, and of course tripped right over me, head first. I rolled over, with my legs waving wildly; the basket upset and scattered the flowers in all directions, and we both screamed at the top of our voices.

It was at this point that a man came round the corner, and nearly fell over us as well.

"What on earth . . . !" he began; but by this time we had sorted ourselves out, and were sitting up.

"Sorry!" said Philip, rubbing his nose.

"You tripped over me," I remarked indignantly.

"Well, you shouldn't have squatted down like that," protested Philip.

"Well, you shouldn't have had your head in the air!" I argued.

"Well, I was watching a skylark," explained my brother peaceably, "and, oh, listen!—I can hear it now!"

He sat in the middle of the path, listening with a rapt expression on his face, his hands clasped tightly together. He had quite forgotten the presence of the tall man, who stood watching him in utter astonishment.

"Are you interested in birds?" asked the man suddenly.

"I'm extremely interested in them," replied Philip, coming out of his dream and lifting serious blue eyes to his questioner. "Are you?"

"Very," answered the man soberly. "I have all sorts

of birds nesting in this garden. I'll show you some if you get up—unless you and your sister wish to sit in the middle of the path all the afternoon."

Philip jumped to his feet and walked away with the man. I gathered up the flowers and followed; they were already deep in conversation on the subject of golden-crested wrens.

We had a very happy half-hour, for he showed us four or five rare nests. Then, when we had been all round the garden, he took us on to the verandah and gave us each a drink of lemonade; and as we drank it, he suddenly remarked, "By the way, why did you come?"

Philip had quite forgotten our real errand, and looked quite startled for a moment. So I answered for him, holding out the basket.

"We came to sell flowers," I explained, "but we fell over. Would you like to buy some?"

He selected three bunches of withered cowslips.

"Is this how you earn your living?" he asked gravely.

"Oh, no," I replied, "not really; we wanted to earn some money for something very particular, so we thought we'd sell some flowers—but nobody seems to want them."

"Nonsense!" said the man. "Cowslips are my favor-

ite flowers. I'd pay a lot for a scent like that,"—and he
pressed fifty cents into my hand.

Philip went rather pink. Then, laying his hand on
the man's sleeve, he said earnestly, "We should like to
give them to you. You have given us such a lovely
afternoon, and . . . and . . . we are very much obliged to
you."

The last words came out with a rush, as though he
was reading a speech. The man's eyes twinkled, but he
still spoke gravely.

"Not at all," he replied. "It's been a pleasure to meet
you, and I should like your little sister to keep the fifty
cents. You have an extraordinary knowledge of birds
for one so young, and I should like you to come again."

I put the fifty cents in my pocket in a great hurry. I
was dreadfully afraid the man would take Philip at his
word, but he didn't. He walked to the gate with us, and
we all shook hands and said, "Thank-you." Then he
turned back up the drive and we stood once again in
the road.

"Let's go home," said Philip.

"All right," I agreed. "Fifty cents isn't bad for a first
day, and we will try again tomorrow."

But Philip did not answer; he was walking down the
road in a happy dream. He had been in a paradise.

Chapter 7

AN UNFORTUNATE TEA-PARTY

WE WENT OUT flower-selling nearly every afternoon after that, for a week, and earned nearly four dollars. We never again met anyone quite so nice as the bird man, but quite a lot of people seemed pleased with our flowers and bought bunches. They looked better, too, because we remembered to put them in water overnight instead of selling them at once, and the basket of fresh, wild bunches made a good show.

We took Terry into our confidence, and he did not mind at all; in fact, he helped us quite a lot, for he had a gift of selecting the right colors and arranging them to perfection. In order that Aunt Margaret should not see the flowers, we kept the bucket by the gap in the hedge, and Terry would sometimes arrive there late in the evenings and add a few of his finds to ours. We had shown him our private gap as a mark of friendship, and he used to creep in and out like a small weasel, and leave notes for us, stuck on the apple boughs. His spelling was shaky, but that did not worry us at all—and anyhow we had invented a code, in case Uncle Peter ever found them when attending to the hens. Aunt Margaret we felt quite safe about; she never went into the orchard.

Most mornings we found a scrap of paper which said, "Cum to △—bring ooooo." This meant that Terry would be waiting for us at the wigwam, and would require feeding; and where Terry commanded, we always obeyed. Aunt Margaret almost gave up the unequal struggle of trying to make me help in the house, and I became really gifted at getting out of doing my jobs. If I ever had a twinge of conscience about her tired and rather sad face, I managed to forget it the minute I had dived through the gap and was out in the world again.

It was toward the end of the week, when we were sitting at dinner, that my aunt remarked:

"I'm going out to tea this afternoon, Philip and Ruth, and I shall not be back till about six. You may take yours out, and not come back till supper, if you like."

We both *did* like, very much, and we kicked each other joyfully under the table.

"Who are you going out to tea with, Auntie?" inquired Philip, who always took a polite interest in other people's affairs.

"With an old friend of mine who has come to live here just lately," answered my aunt. "Later on, I should like to introduce you to her; she is very fond of children, and has often asked about you. She knew your mother, too."

"Will she ask us out to tea, too?" I inquired with interest. I liked going out to tea because we always had such nice things to eat.

"If she did you would have to behave yourself better than you usually do," replied my aunt dryly, and I frowned and wriggled with annoyance. Why should she always spoil even nice, good things like going out to tea with silly remarks like that? Of course I always behaved nicely out to tea! I was far too shy not to, and in any case it was rather fun having grown-ups say how well-mannered we were; quite a change, too, as far as I was concerned.

Dinner over, my aunt hurried me off to the kitchen to help dry the dishes, which I did at lightning speed and made off the instant I'd finished. Aunt Margaret called after me to come back and put the cloth away tidily, but I pretended not to hear, and rushed through the front door. I knew she could not possibly catch me, for I was as fleet-footed as a little rabbit, and I hoped she might have forgotten by the evening. Going out to tea would drive it out of her memory.

Philip was waiting near the gap, looking rather anxious, with the basket in his hand.

"Come along," he said, "we must get well away before Auntie starts. We might meet her—and we forgot to ask which way she was going."

"Oh, I think she's going down the town way," I answered carelessly. "I heard her say something to Uncle Peter about it—someone she was going to see down Beech Road."

"But perhaps it was somebody else," objected Philip.

"No, no," I replied reassuringly, "it was sure to be the same one. She doesn't go and see many people; she's too busy."

Philip chewed a piece of grass thoughtfully.

"She's always working, isn't she?" he remarked at last. "Sometimes I think we might help her a bit more than we do. After all, it's quite kind of her to have us to live with her; we're not her children."

"Oh, I don't know," I answered quickly, for this sort of talk was not at all to my liking. "I help with the drying and dusting sometimes, and you do the wood for Uncle Peter, and we both pick fruit in summer, and shell peas and things. After all we're not grown-ups.

Children shouldn't have to work on holidays. We do quite enough work in the term."

But I could see by the look on Philip's face that he was not quite satisfied, so I changed the subject as soon as possible.

We went down a country road today, to a collection of rather pretty cottages mostly inhabited by retired, elderly ladies. The boughs of the hedges were weighed down with heavy blossom. Underneath, on the banks, buttercups, vetches, dead nettles, speed-wells, and cow parsley grew in sweet-scented riot, all stretching up toward the sunshine. It was the high tide of early summer, and the birds sang as though they would burst their throttles with song. It was a peaceful sort of day on which no one would expect anything to happen; and so we were taken completely by surprise, never dreaming that the afternoon would turn out as it did.

The old ladies were unusually nice, too, and at the first four houses everyone bought something, and we earned over fifty cents. Most old ladies fell in love with Philip and did whatever he wanted; I suppose it was his blue eyes and his polite, serious way of speaking. One of them patted him on the head and called him "Little man," which he did not like at all, and one of them gave us a chocolate each, which we liked very much indeed. She was a rosy old lady, the color of a russet apple, and she said Philip reminded her of her grandson. He replied in his sweetest voice that she reminded him of his grandmother, which pleased her greatly, and caused her to run indoors and produce the chocolate.

"Philip," I said severely, when we were outside the gate, "you haven't seen Granny for years, and I don't believe you can remember her at all."

"Oh, yes, I can," he answered contentedly, licking away at his chocolate; "she had white hair and smelled of mothballs."

"But this one had grey hair and smelled of kippered herring," I argued, "at least, the house did—she was frying some for her tea."

"Oh, well," said my brother placidly, "it doesn't matter; she could easily remind me of Granny just by being an old lady; they're all the same—let's have tea."

We wandered up a lane, and sat on a gate looking over a radiant buttercup field, where sleepy brown cows chewed their cud and switched their tails lazily. We munched our bread and jam as peacefully as the cows and almost as silently, for Philip was not really a talkative boy. He had a good deal to think about, as he sometimes told me when I chattered.

Finished, we lay down in the grass and drank from a pipe, which was spurting water out of the bank. It wasn't very nice, and I thought it had an unpleasant flavor; Philip drank a great deal, and then remarked that he only hoped it wasn't the drains.

It was only four o'clock, so we decided to go back to the road and try some more cottages. We were going to do our best today, and then go back to Terry and the woods tomorrow, for we were getting a little tired of flower-selling; still, it was encouraging to be finishing up so well, and on reaching the road we approached the next cottage hopefully enough.

It was a very nice one, long, low and built of grey stone, with beds of tulips massed against it. It stood on a little rise of ground and a pink and white apple orchard sloped away from one side of it. We pattered up the path and along to the front door; on our way we passed under a window, and heard the clink of china and the sound of ladies' voices. It sounded as if some sort of a tea-party was going on, and ladies at tea-parties are usually in rather a good mood, as Philip wisely remarked.

We rang the bell, and the drawing room door opened immediately. A young lady came out and stood looking at us for a moment before asking us what we wanted. When we held out the basket and asked her to buy some flowers, her face dimpled with amusement; I had noticed that a good many people looked amused when we told them we were flower-sellers, but I never quite understood why.

"Wait a minute," she said, instead of answering our question: "I must ask my mother, and then you must come in and show us what you've picked."

She disappeared into the drawing room, and we heard her merry laugh as she told her mother about us.

"Such a picturesque little couple, pretending to be flower-sellers," we heard her say. "The boy has a face like an angel, and the girl looks like a little wild gypsy. You must see them for yourselves; I'll bring them in."

She reappeared, all smiles, and held out her hand.

"Come in a moment," she said, "and show my mother and aunt your basket; I'm sure they would like to buy some cowslips. You shall have a cookie each, too; we're just having tea."

We trotted in after her, suspecting nothing, and then both stopped dead in the doorway, transfixed with horror.

There were four chairs placed round a little table in the window so that the ladies were sitting with their backs to us. In the first chair sat a tall, elderly lady who was evidently the mother, for she was pouring; next to her sat the aunt, and next to her was the empty seat which was about to be occupied by the young lady.

And next to that was a high-backed armchair, with

large sides, and from the depths of it came the perfectly unmistakable voice of my aunt.

"The little girl is very unruly," said the voice, confidentially. "I shall be only too glad when her mother comes and takes her off my hands."

"Run!" I whispered to Philip. "Oh, Phil, run quick!"

But Philip in his usual slow fashion had not yet realized what had happened; he stood there blinking as though he were in some puzzling dream. I knew he would be several minutes making up his mind to run, and by that time it would be too late, so I cast about in my mind for some other way of escape.

There was one slender hope; if we walked in and stood behind my aunt's chair, it was quite impossible for her to see us without doing extraordinary gymnastics, for the chair was very big. If we were required to speak, she would certainly know it was us; however, it was our only chance; as the young lady was beckoning us to come forward, wondering why we were hesitating, I took Philip's hand and led him straight to the only safe spot in the room.

Old Mrs. Sheridan and her sister smiled and tried to put us at our ease. She held out her hand for a bunch of cowslips; I took two steps forward, leaned right over, thrust them at her, and went back to my hiding-place like a frightened rabbit to its burrow. The girl looked rather surprised, for we had not seemed shy on the doorstep; yet here we were behaving in the most peculiar fashion. Philip was standing like a stuffed image, with his mouth open, looking as though he were seeing a ghost.

"What beautiful big flowers!" said Mrs. Sheridan, examining the clusters, "we shall have to go exploring and find some, too; whereabouts did you pick these, children?"

There was dead silence; neither of us dared speak. I heard a rustle in the armchair as though my aunt was about to turn round and examine these strange dumb specimens behind her—and if her head suddenly appeared over the top I knew I should scream. So I replied, in a hoarse whisper, "In the hollow, by the stream."

"By the stream," repeated Mrs. Sheridan. "Yes, I might have known these had grown near water; I shall certainly buy a bunch; fetch my purse, Isabel, and give these two children a cookie each before they go."

The girl held out the plate, but to reach it we should have to walk out in the open; we shook our heads frantically, and lifting imploring eyes, but she merely thought we were being polite.

"Come along," she said, laughing, "they're very nice."

Hopelessly I took two steps forward, and leaned over as far as I could to grab two cookies; but as I did so I saw my aunt's hat move, and I leaped backwards; in so doing, I bumped into a small cake stand and sent it flying.

At which point my aunt's head came right round the arm of the chair, and she saw me.

I can only dimly remember what happened next; I heard my aunt say, "Philip and Ruth, what is the meaning of this?" in a voice that reminded me of a bugle blast, and I heard Mrs. Sheridan say, "Pick them up, Isabel—they are butter-side down, all over the carpet—don't let them get trodden in." I saw Philip move back and trip over Isabel, who was picking up buttered buns, and I noticed that her face looked as though she were trying not to laugh. I remember everybody apologizing for everybody, and my aunt saying she could not understand it, a great many times, and Mrs. Sheridan saying it was nothing to worry about, and we were to forget all about it.

The next thing that comes back to me was my aunt's turning to us when the commotion had died down, and telling us she was taking us home to punish us most severely; but before we went we were to come forward

and tell Mrs. Sheridan how sorry we were for behaving
so badly.

Philip had regained his senses by now, and he
stepped forward immediately and looked up into Mrs.
Sheridan's face. He was truly sorry for having spoiled
such a nice tea-party, especially when Aunt Margaret
went to so few, and he said so, so earnestly and politely
that everyone was charmed; even my aunt looked
pleased, and if only she could have stopped there, all
would have ended peacefully; but now she turned to
me and asked me coldly what I had to say for myself.

I don't quite understand to this day why I was so
angry, but while Philip was talking I had decided that
my aunt was an idiot; there was no need to have recognized and owned us—we should never have shown we
belonged to her, and then no one would have known.
Therefore, I argued, she had brought all this trouble on
herself, and here we were being told *we* were naughty,
in front of everyone—and we weren't naughty—why
shouldn't we sell flowers? Anyone would think we were
stealing!

All this was flashing through my rebellious little
heart when my aunt spoke to me; for answer, I stuck
my hands in my pockets and stamped my muddy boot.

"I'm not a bit sorry," I stormed. "We're not doing
anything wrong, and no one called us naughty till we

met you. We've earned the money and it belongs to us, and we shall go on doing it if we want. You always spoil everything, Aunt Margaret."

My aunt went quite white; never in my worst moments at home had I spoken to her like this, and here I was disgracing us all in somebody else's drawing room. I suddenly felt terrified and miserable, and ran out into the garden, leaving them all standing looking at each other.

I wanted to dash on, but realized that they might think I was running away, and I was far too proud to run away. So I walked off toward home with my hands in my pockets, and my head held very high in the air; I knew my aunt and Philip were coming down the hill behind me, so I pretended to whistle, but I was too miserable to keep it up for long. When I reached home I went and stared out of the kitchen window, and tried to whistle again. I wanted to look as if nothing had happened and as though I didn't care if it had; above all, I wasn't going to be sorry.

My aunt came in slowly, as though she was very, very tired; she crossed the room and stood beside me, looking out of the window.

"Ruth," she said, rather heavily, "I'm not going to punish you, because it doesn't seem to do much good, but I've been thinking it out on the way home. I don't seem to be able to manage you, or bring you up as I should; you have ten days' more holiday, and then if they can take you, I am going to send you to boarding school. Your mother suggested it at Christmas, but I wanted to keep you then. Of course, it will be a big extra expense, but anything is better than have you grow up as selfish and obstinate and ill-mannered as you are now."

She turned away without looking at me, and I went on staring out of the window; I felt as though the whole world was falling down round me, and I wanted to run to Philip, and bury my face in his jersey and cry, as I used to when a tiny girl. But Philip had been sent straight upstairs to bed, and I was alone.

"I shan't go," I said, in what was meant to be a defiant voice, but which only sounded small and shaky.

"You won't be asked," replied my aunt, quietly.

There was a long silence, and I stood perfectly still, thinking furiously. Then I spoke again in the same small, trembling voice that tried so hard to be proud:

"Very well," I announced, "I shall run away, and I shan't come back," and with that I ran straight out of the door, and into the road.

My aunt took no notice. It was very early, and I

often rushed off like this in a temper. No doubt I would come back before dark. What she did was to sigh heavily and go slowly up to her room.

Chapter 8

RUNNING AWAY

I DID NOT STOP for a minute when I got out into the road. It did not matter to me where I went so long as I got away, and in my angry heart I decided that I would never, never go back again. I would be a gypsy's little girl, or get some kind lady to adopt me, or ask someone to let me be his little servant. Then perhaps Aunt Margaret would be sorry. I knew Uncle Peter would miss me when he came home every night, and of course Philip would be dreadfully sad; at the thought of Philip my eyes brimmed over. I went on running and running with the tears streaming down my cheeks, quite breathless, and sobbing.

I had chosen the white country road that led away into Herefordshire, between young wheat fields and banks of flowers. It was a pretty, lonely road rising up over hills and dipping down into valleys, winding and twisting so that you always wanted to go on and see what lay around the next corner. Now it was at its most beautiful, with the evening light shining on sloping buttercup meadows and the shadows of the trees long and quiet across the gold. But I noticed nothing, and being quite out of breath, I settled down into a trot; so I trotted on and on, not caring where I went, and much too miserable to wonder what was going to become of me.

"You're going away to boarding school." I kept whispering the horrid words to myself, and trying to take it all in. I saw myself going away in disgrace, alone in a train to a building which I imagined would be rather like a jail. And I imagined Terry and Philip sitting in the wigwam together, with the birds singing and the foxgloves sprouting and the wild roses uncurling—and I should not be there. Then other pictures seemed to dance before my eyes: Philip kneeling alone at the bedroom window with the sun rising—and my little bed empty; Philip lying on his tummy in the hayfields, writing his book—and I should not be there to draw the pictures.

It was quiet all around me as I trotted along; I had met no one, and except for the cries of birds going to bed and my own sobbing, the world had seemed quite silent. But now I suddenly became aware of the sound of children's voices and the barking of a dog. So I rubbed away the tears with the back of my hand and looked about me.

I had reached the entrance to a village where I had been once or twice before. It was a very little village; only a few cottages, a white square school, a village shop, and a church. It nestled in a dip of the low hills just where the country road met a larger main road with a signpost.

I stood for some little time wondering what to do; I did not want to walk through the village just yet, for I knew that everyone would think I had been crying. Besides, I was hot and dreadfully tired, and my head was beginning to ache; I wanted to sit somewhere cool and quiet, where I could rest, and think where to go next. I looked all round me, and then realized that I was standing by a little brown wooden gate that led into the churchyard, and the church door was open. No one was likely to go into church as late as this. Even if they did I could crouch down in a pew, and they would not see me; so I went up the path between rows of quiet gravestones, reading the names as I went.

Once stone interested me specially, and I stopped to read it again; it was a little white cross, marking a garden of forget-me-nots; on it was graven, "Jane Collins, aged nine years; went to be with the Lord, April 5th, 1900."

I read it several times, and then shivered at the thought of poor little Jane Collins who had had to rise up at the strange call of Death, and leave this world on an April day with its sunshine and its lambs, its singing birds and first flowers. Death had always seemed a distant thing, to be thought about by old people and ministers, but Jane Collins was only nine years old when she went to be with the Lord. What if I, aged nine, had suddenly to go and be with the Lord; what would He say to me about all my tempers, and the lies I'd told, and the times I'd run away instead of helping, and the dust under the carpet? It would be far, far worse than going to boarding school; for the first time in my life I began to feel really frightened about being so naughty.

I walked on into the church porch, and peeped cautiously inside; it was quite empty, so I slipped through the door and began wandering round looking at the inscriptions, and the pictures, and the daffodils in vases; one thing pleased me most of all—and that was the evening light streaming through the stained-glass windows and falling in colored patterns on the floor, making a sort of fairy track all up the western side of the church.

As I stood watching, it suddenly came over me how dreadfully tired I was. The church was so quiet and cool and friendly, with its sunset light and its daffodils, that I thought I would lie down and rest a little before deciding what to do next. I collected some foot-stools, made a little mattress, wrapped myself up in an old black robe that hung near the door, then cuddled down inside one of the pews where I could watch the beautiful patterns and think things out.

But I had not realized how sleepy I was; I had been out in the open air all day; I had been very frightened and very angry and very miserable, and I had run nearly three miles on a warm spring evening. All these things were enough to make any little girl dog-tired; in fact, I was so tired that I hardly remember laying my head down before all my cares melted away and I knew I couldn't keep awake any longer.

But just as I was dropping off, I thought I saw Jane Collins standing in the sunset light of the west window, pointing upward along the golden rays. She was a little girl just like me, with dark braids and a pinafore and blue socks, and the moment I saw her face I knew I had made a mistake in pitying her, for never before, either in dreams or real life, had I seen one look so radiantly happy. Her arms were full of Easter flowers, and somehow I knew that they would never fade or die. Then the light grew dim and blurred and I fell into a deep, deep sleep.

When I awoke I was lying in the dark, and for a long time I could not imagine where I was. I was very stiff, and cold, and sore, for the footstools had come apart and I was lying partly on the stone floor. I thought I must be having a nightmare, and called out for Philip, but my voice echoed horribly through the church. I dared not call again, so I snuggled down, shivering under the black robe, and tried to remember what it was all about.

Very gradually it came back to me; I had run away; Aunt Margaret was going to send me to boarding school; I had been very naughty, and no one would ever forgive me, and nobody loved me—except Philip, and I should not see Philip for months and months. Then I realized that I was all alone in a great empty church and there might be thieves or rats. Perhaps it was only about midnight, and I should have to wait hours and hours till morning. Perhaps I should die of cold and hunger and have to go and be with the Lord like Jane Collins. Then I remembered my dream, and felt slightly comforted, until it struck me that Jane Collins had probably been a very good little girl, with nothing to be afraid of when she went to be with the Lord.

But I had everything to be afraid of; my aunt had called me a wicked girl, and now, lying there crying in

the dark, I believed her for the first time. I kept
remembering more and more times when I had deceived her, and disobeyed her, and been rude to her. I
wondered whether she was still waiting for me to come
home, and whether they had come out to look for me.
Perhaps they hadn't cared, and had gone to bed, and
were all lying asleep under warm blankets while I lay
dying of cold. At this thought I felt so sorry for myself
that I broke out into fresh, hopeless sobbing.

All this time my face was buried in my arms, but I
was getting so stiff, and the floor felt so hard, that I sat
up and changed my position; directly I lifted my face I
found that a wonderful thing had happened. The day
was beginning to dawn, and a gray light was stealing
through the eastern windows on the other side of the
church; the darkness had scattered, and with it all my
terrors and nightmares. I gave a great sigh of relief,
and sat quite still with my small white face turned
toward the morning.

As I sat there waiting and listening, the dreadful
silence was broken by the clear call of a bird, and I
realized with a thrill of joy that the world was waking
up again after the terrible night. Then another bird
awoke and answered, then another, until it seemed as
though every bird must be singing itself hoarse. As I sat
listening, the gray light gave place to gold, and the

whole bird choir seemed to go mad with joy: the sun
was rising, and morning had come again.

The relief was so great that I did not want to move. I
forgot that I was cold and hungry and only remembered that the night was over, and that I was no longer
alone, because the birds had awakened. Soon I would
slip out of the church and run home to Philip, but for
the moment I was content to sit and listen.

I did not sit and listen for long, for somehow my
head fell over on to the footstools and I dropped fast
asleep again. When I awoke the next time it was very
suddenly, for the church was flooded with light, and
there were heavy footsteps coming up the aisle.

I sat quite still and waited as the footsteps came
nearer, and then my curiosity got the better of me; I
crawled to the edge of the pew and peered over. It was
the minister; he was walking slowly up the church
aisle, looking up at the eastern windows. He need not
have seen me at all, for his head was turned away and I
was small enough to creep under the seat; I was just
about to do this, for I did not want to be seen. Children
were not allowed to sleep in churches, I was sure, and
there was a Police Station just down the road. But I had
been lying all night in a drafty church with my legs on
a stone floor, and I had caught a cold, so I was only half
out of sight when a dreadful thing happened.

I sneezed!

I tried to stop, but it was no use; out it came with a loud explosion, and the minister jumped. Then he came and looked at the pew; there he saw half a little girl, wrapped up in a robe, sticking out from under the seat.

He said nothing, but came and sat down; then he leaned over and spoke very gently:

"Come out," he said. "There's no need to hide under the seat. I don't mind children in my church."

I uncurled slowly, sat down on the seat beside him, and looked up into his face. He was not very young and not very old, and his eyes were blue and kind. He reminded me of the old shepherd, somehow, only he was not wrinkled and whiskery. It was just that he was the sort of man I was not afraid of talking to.

"I couldn't help being here," I explained. "I came in last night when the door was open, and I went to sleep by mistake; I put on your clothes because I was cold, but I didn't mean to stay all night. Only when I woke up the first time it was too dark to move, and when I woke up the second time it was morning."

He looked rather startled. "Do you mean that you have been here all night?" he asked. "Whatever is your mother thinking? We must let her know where you are at once."

I sat silent a moment, twisting my hands together. I had a sudden funny feeling that I wanted to tell someone all about it, and I thought this man would do. Quite uninvited, I leaned my weary head against his shoulder.

"It's not my mother," I whispered, "it's my aunt; I wouldn't have done it with my mother; I've been very, very naughty and she's going to send me away to boarding school because she can't manage me, and I didn't want to go, so I ran away, and here I am."

I looked up to see if he was very shocked, but he didn't seem to be so. He just looked very interested and rather sorry for me.

"I'm glad you told me that," he said gravely, "and I should like you to tell me a great deal more about it. But first of all we must tell your aunt where you are; then, perhaps, when she knows you're safe, she will let you stay a little, and we can talk. Do you have a phone?"

We did, and I knew the number.

"Good," said my friend. "We'll ring your aunt at the parsonage, and tell her all about it."

I put my small hand into his large one and we walked out of the church together. The world was perfectly radiant with song and light and color, but I knew it must be very early morning, because the flower petals were still closed.

"Why did you come to church so early?" I asked suddenly.

"I came to pray," answered the minister. "I often come out early, because everything looks so beautiful. Don't you think that these buttercups are enough to make anyone feel good and happy?"

I looked at the buttercups but I did not feel happy, and I was quite certain I should never be good.

Chapter 9

I MAKE A NEW FRIEND

WE WENT INTO the parsonage and he took me straight to his study. It was a big sunny room, full of books, and while I sat and rested in a big arm-chair he went to telephone. He was gone a long time, and having nothing else to do I wandered around the room looking at the pictures; they were mostly photographs and not very interesting, but there was one that I liked so much that I moved my chair over in front of it so that I could look at it.

I have the picture now. It is the picture of a sheep lost on a rocky mountain-side. Overhead hovers a fierce bird, waiting for it to die, and the sheep looks up and cries to be rescued. Someone has heard its cry, for the shepherd with his crook is leaning over the precipice; in another moment he will pick it up and carry it safe home in his arms.

I was so interested in the picture that I never noticed

that the minister had come back. Now he stood in front
of me with a tray which he laid down beside me.

"I've telephoned your aunt," he said. "She's been
very anxious about you, and the police and your uncle
have been out looking for you all night. However, now
she knows you're safe she doesn't mind your staying to
breakfast with me. Afterward you must run home and
tell her how sorry you are."

I fell upon the tray of food with a tremendous appetite, for I had had nothing to eat since the day before. It
was such a nice breakfast, too, with a boiled egg and
strawberry jam and a teapot all to myself. I munched
away most contentedly; he sat down on the sofa while I
ate my breakfast, and we talked. I told him all about
Philip and Terry, and the bird book, and the wigwam,
and the camera, and the flower-selling. He asked a
great many questions, and seemed really interested.

But when I had finished my last mouthful of bread
and jam, I realized that now I should probably be sent
straight home. I didn't want to go just yet for I thought
my new friend was one of the nicest men I had ever
met except perhaps Mr. Tandy, the old shepherd. So I
went over and sat down beside him on the sofa; once
again I found myself staring at the picture on the wall.

Isn't that a nice picture?" I remarked. "It reminds
me of the shepherd at home. One of his lambs escaped,

like the one on the picture, and he went to look for it. I went, too; we looked for ever so long, and then we found it all tangled up in a thorn bush, crying, and it took Mr. Tandy ages to get it out; his hands got all scratched to bits in the thorns."

My friend was looking at the picture, also; he did not answer for a minute.

"Ruth," he said suddenly, "how did the lamb get into such a place? Why did he ever get lost?"

"Well," I replied, "I suppose he ran away; they often do."

"Yes," went on the minister—and he was speaking very earnestly now. "But why did he run away? He had a kind shepherd and a very nice green field. Why didn't he stay there?"

"Well," I answered thoughtfully, "I expect he thought it looked nicer outside, and went to see. Then I expect he got lost, and when he wanted to go back he just couldn't find the way."

"You're quite right," said my new friend. "Just look at the lamb in the picture. I expect he had been trying to find his way back all night; but he was lost, and the farther he went, the steeper the rocks became, and the more hopeless he felt. So I think he stopped trying at last, and just stood quite still at the edge of the precipice; and what did he do then, Ruth?"

I looked up at him; I was beginning to understand that he was not talking about a real sheep any longer.

"I don't know," I whispered, rather shyly.

"Well, then, I'll tell you," went on my friend. "I think he looks around and sees a precipice underneath him, and big rocks above him, and he says to himself, 'It's no good, I can't possibly get back by myself. There's only one Person who can take me home—and that's the Shepherd.' So he opens his mouth and gives a little cry; the Shepherd has been waiting all night for that little cry; directly He hears it He leans over and picks up the lamb, and carries it safely back to His own pasture—and I don't know who is the happier, the lamb or the Shepherd."

My eyes were fixed on him; I knew now that he was talking about me.

"I ran away, too, and got lost last night, didn't I?" I whispered.

"You did," answered the minister, "and, do you know, when I found you hiding in the church and you told me that you'd run away and you didn't know how to be good, I thought to myself, 'Here's one of God's lost lambs trying to get back by herself'—and you'll never do it, Ruth. There's only one Person who can take you back into God's way and keep you there, and that is the Lord Jesus Christ, who called Himself the Good Shepherd."

"Then why doesn't He do it?" I asked.

"Because you are still trying to get back without Him," came the answer. "You tell me you try to be good, but you keep being naughty instead. Well, every time you are naughty you are getting a little bit farther away from God's way, and a little bit more lost than you were before. What you have to do is to stop trying to make yourself good; you've got to tell the Shepherd that you are quite lost, and ask Him to find you and take you back into God's way, and to make you one of His own obedient lambs."

"Will He really do it?" I asked.

"Ruth," said the minister suddenly, "how old are you?"

"Nine," I answered, wondering what that had to do with it.

"Well, then, He's been loving you and looking for you for nine whole years; don't you think He'll be glad to hear you call to Him, when He's been waiting for such a long time?"

I sat very still, thinking hard.

"Is it really all I've got to do to be good?" I asked at last. "I thought it was very difficult to be good."

"It's all you must do at first," he answered; "that's

the wonderful part. You see, the Good Shepherd has done it all for you. He took away sin when He died for sinners on the cross, so that you can be forgiven without any punishment. You told me that your friend's hands got dreadfully torn and scratched as he rescued that lamb—but he lifted the lamb out of the thorns without hurting it at all. And in just the same way the Good Shepherd was wounded and hurt when He came to look for you; He has done everything, and all you've to do is to say, 'Thank you,' and to believe that His wounded hands can lift you up and carry you back to God's fold when you ask him."

"And what happens then?" I asked. "Shall I always be good after that?"

He smiled.

"You won't always be good all at once," he replied, "but you will always belong to the Good Shepherd, and He will begin to teach you how to be good. He will often speak to you in your heart, and you must learn to listen to His voice; when He speaks you must always obey. And you must learn to talk to Him about everything, too; we call it praying, but really it means sharing everything with the Shepherd."

Once more we sat still for a long time. At last the minister spoke:

"I have to go to my church now," he said gently,

"and you must go home, or your aunt will think you've run away somewhere else. Before you go I'm going to give you a copy of that picture for your very own. Take it with you and look at it often, and each time you look at it remember that you are that lost lamb and that the Good Shepherd is waiting to find you as soon as you ask Him. One other thing—have you a Bible of your own?"

I said I had a very nice Bible in my drawer at home.

"Then when you reach home find the Gospel of Luke, and read a little bit every night. It will tell you the story of the Shepherd and how He came to earth to look for lost sheep. And when you've finished it, read the other Gospels."

He had opened a drawer and produced a postcard-size copy of the picture on the wall. I took it with shining eyes, and whispered my thanks.

I followed him out, holding my new treasure tightly in both hands; he came to the front gate and stood watching me as I set out along the road. When I had gone about a hundred yards I turned around and ran back. I stood on tiptoe and pulled his head down so that I could whisper in his ear.

"Shall I come back and tell you when it's happened?" I asked.

He nodded. "I was hoping you would," he admitted.

"I shall always be glad to see you, so come whenever you like."

So I left him and turned the corner. The road ahead of me led back home, and at the thought of home my heart beat rather fast. What would my aunt and uncle say to me, and what should I say to them?

But I did not worry much, for I had more important things to think about. In my hand was the picture, and in my heart was a great resolve. I would find some quiet place far away from everyone, and before I went back home I would ask the Good Shepherd to find me and make me one of His lambs.

I was very particular about the spot; the cornfields would not do, because I could be seen from the road, and I wanted to be quite alone. I trotted on until I came to that part where the road ran between woods, and in late summer the boughs nearly met overhead; here I climbed the bank and slipped in and out among the trees till I had reached a little clearing right away from any path. The moss grew thick on the ground and clematis vine hung in curtains round me; here I knelt down and felt as though I were in some secret chapel, far away from the world.

I looked again at my picture, but at first I dared not pray. I felt as if my whole life was going to depend on the next few moments. What if I spoke and nothing happened? What if the Shepherd had gone away and was not listening any more?

Then I spoke aloud to the Good Shepherd. I told Him about my naughtiness, and how I couldn't be good by myself; I told Him I was sorry because I'd kept Him waiting so long; and then I asked Him to forgive me and find me and pick me up in His arms, and never to let me run away from Him again.

I waited, perfectly still, for my answer, almost expecting to feel His gentle arms thrown round me: and what happened? I heard nothing, and I felt nothing, but I knew that my prayer was heard. I could not possibly have put it into words, but I knew that love and forgiveness were around about me as certainly as the sunlight and the quiet air—knew at that instant that I was sought and loved and found.

I was so happy that I stayed where I was for a long time, as though by moving I might break the spell. I was not only happy, I was grateful, too; I remembered how long He had waited, and I thought of Mr. Tandy's poor bleeding hands, and remembered how the hands of the Shepherd had been wounded when He died on the cross for me. I did not understand it all, but the minister had said that the Bible made it very plain, and I believed him. So I folded my hands again and tried to thank Him.

Then it suddenly struck me that I was supposed to be going home; my aunt was waiting for me. So I left my outdoor church, and went back to the road.

But I walked very slowly; would they be very angry with me? I wondered; and, worst of all, would I be naughty and rude again? My rudeness seemed to come out whether I wanted it to or not. If I was naughty now everything would be spoiled.

Then I remembered something else; the Shepherd had picked me up in His arms, and I could tell Him everything if He was really as close to me as all that. So I told Him all about it as I trotted home, and somehow all my happiness came back to me. I was not alone any longer.

I swallowed hard as I opened the front door and slipped inside—a dirty, scared, untidy little figure clasping my hands tightly together in the hall. I had no idea what I was going to say to my aunt; only to myself I kept whispering the words, "Even if I'm punished, help me to be good."

My aunt suddenly appeared at the kitchen door, and we both stood looking at each other in silence.

But the loving Shepherd had found me, and when we first come to know His love He begins to make us more loving, too. As I stood stiffly in the hall something happened to my hard little heart that I had not expected. I suddenly ran forward and flung myself into my aunt's arms.

"I'm sorry, Auntie," I whispered; "I will try to be good. And please, please don't send me to boarding school. I want to stay with you here, and I'll never, never run away or be naughty again."

My aunt, kneeling, pressed my tear-stained cheek against hers and held me close to her. Then she smoothed back my tangled hair and kissed me.

"My poor little girl," she whispered back, "I don't want to send you away if I can possibly help it; we'll try again."

Then she took my hand and led me to the table in the kitchen, where I sat down and ate a whole second breakfast to make up for the supper I missed the night before.

Chapter 10

THE SQUIRREL'S NEST

I CAUGHT A BAD COLD from sleeping in the church, and had to go to bed for three days. Philip stayed with me most of the time, so we put in a lot of work on the bird book. When we were tired of drawing and writing we talked. He was never tired of hearing about my night in the church, and I was flattered to hear how much everybody had missed me.

"I don't think Auntie or Uncle went to bed all night," Philip told me. "I couldn't go to sleep either. I thought you might be dead, and I was crying and crying in bed; then I went downstairs and I found Auntie crying in the kitchen; we had a drink of cocoa together, and she gave me a chocolate cookie, and we sat by the fire and talked."

I felt rather hurt that Philip should have found such comfort in a chocolate cookie when I might have been lying dead in a ditch.

"What did you talk about?" I said, hoping it had been about me.

"Oh, lots of things," answered my brother cheerfully. "I said perhaps you'd been drowned in the brook. Auntie said she thought you were probably just hiding, and she might send you to boarding school as a punishment, and I said I thought it was a bad idea."

"Why?" I inquired hopefully.

"Because I shouldn't have anyone to play with on Saturdays," he explained. "I said I thought it wouldn't be any use, because you would run away at once."

"And what did she say, then?"

"She said you wouldn't be able to. So I said it would be a pity to send you to boarding school, because I should probably have a nervous breakdown."

"Whatever's that?" I asked, with great interest.

"Oh, it's an illness you get when people do things you don't like. I heard Auntie talking about someone who had a nervous breakdown because the cook went away. So I said I would have one if you went away."

"Like measles?" I asked; measles was the only illness I had ever had, and I thought it of great importance.

"Oh, I don't know," answered Philip. "I don't think it has spots, but it doesn't matter, anyhow; you're not going now, but you'll have to be awfully careful about being good, because once she's thought of it she may think of it again."

I was silent. I hadn't told anyone yet about what had happened to me for somehow I did not know how to put it into words. How could I persuade Philip that something had really taken place? There was nothing to show for it, and sometimes, lying there with a sore throat and a stopped-up nose, I began to wonder how much of it was true, or whether perhaps I'd imagined it. And then I would take out my precious picture and look at it until my doubts disappeared. I would bury my face in the pillow and ask the Shepherd to let me feel close to Him again, as I had felt that morning when we had walked home.

There was my Bible, too. When I got home, I un-earthed it from the drawer and started to read it. After much searching I found the chapter Mr. Tandy had read to me about the sheep that was lost; I read it over to myself again and again until I almost knew it by heart. I read the rest of the chapter, too, about the boy who ran away, just like me, and who came home again and said he was sorry, and was forgiven by his father. I thought it was exactly like me and Aunt Margaret; I liked it very much.

I tried to pray, too; I had been taught to say my prayers, but somehow it was different now; before it was just saying words because I thought I ought to, but now I was talking to Someone I knew and who loved me.

It was on my second night in bed that I made a great discovery. Philip had gone down to supper, and I had pulled out my Bible from under my pillow, for I was rather shy of letting anyone see me read it. As I turned the pages of the Gospels, looking for stories, I came to the tenth chapter of John, and the word "Shepherd" caught my eye at once.

I had often heard the chapter read in church and at school, but I had forgotten whereabouts in the Bible it was. Now I read it eagerly, for it was the very thing I was hungering for. Here it was, all over again:

"I am the good shepherd: the good shepherd giveth his life for the sheep." That meant that the Shepherd had come to die on the cross before He could find me.

I did not understand the verses about thieves and robbers, but I understood about the sheep following; that meant being good and doing what the Shepherd said—but what could it mean about "hearing the Shepherd's voice"? The minister had said that Jesus would speak to me, and that I must obey, but although I had been in bed with my eyes shut, listening hard, I could hear nothing. The room seemed perfectly silent, and I did so want the Good Shepherd to say something to me. How could I know His voice if He never spoke to me?

This question troubled me quite a lot that night and next day, until I suddenly had a good idea: I would go and see Mr. Tandy, take him my postal-card and tell him all about what had happened; perhaps he would be able to tell me about the Shepherd's voice.

I was very impatient to get up after this. I was allowed to go down to tea on the fourth day. It was a happy meal, and I went to bed thinking that after all it was much nicer being good. Being naughty was not really worth it; when I went to bed that night I told the Good Shepherd that I was never, never going to be naughty again.

To my relief, the next day was sunny, and after dinner I set off joyously across the fields with Philip. It was a special afternoon because I had not been out for four whole days; also it felt rather precious because the end of the holidays was so near—only five more days, and one of them a Sunday—which did not count. Philip was going to take me to see a squirrel's drey or nest that he and Terry had found in a magpie's nest.

"It's a very difficult tree," explained Philip, "and I don't think you'll be able to climb it, because you're not tall enough, but I'll go up and bring a baby down."

"How will you carry it?" I asked.

"Down my shirt," answered Philip. "You'll see!" And he trotted on with his head in the air, trying to make a willow warbler answer him by chirping down the scale in half tones.

It was a hot, lazy day, and we plunged gratefully into the shade of the woods. The fern was knee high, and cow wheat rambled over the stones and patches. All the trees had sprouted their leaves now, and the sunlight was shut out. The paths were narrowed by the upshootings on each side, so we had to walk single file.

The squirrel's nest was on the topmost fork of a high oak, and the lowest branch was a long way from the ground, higher than I could reach, even on Philip's shoulders. But Philip and Terry could swarm up bare trunks as though they were squirrels themselves. I had tried hard to learn how to do it, and had torn many frocks, and had scraped many layers of skin off my knees and elbows, but so far I had been unsuccessful.

Up went Philip, pressing against the trunk with his strong bare limbs. He pulled himself up on to the lowest branch and began climbing, hand over hand, until he reached the top. The branches were very thin where he stood, a perilous little figure against the sky. Then he stretched up and dipped his hand into the nest.

"Oo!" he called down, "it's like plunging your hand

into a nest full of fur. They are all squirming and wriggling, and trying to bite me."

"Oh, bring one down! Bring one down!" I squealed excitedly. "I want to hold it. Do be quick, Philip!"

But Philip, who was never quick about anything, was slowly and deliberately buttoning it up into his shirt.

"Now," he announced, "I'm coming down."

For a few moments all went well; then there came agitated remarks from the tree.

"He's run round the back, Ruth, and I can't let go. You can't come up and fish him out, can you?"

"I don't think I can reach," I called back. "And, anyhow, does it matter—him going round the back?"

"*Yes,*" answered my brother in deep distress. "He's biting and scratching me dreadfully, and I'm sort of stuck. Do try and come, Ruth!"

The thought of Philip's nice brown back being slowly chewed up was too much for me. I dug my elbows and knees desperately into the bark and swarmed. Crimson in the face, and nearly bursting with effort, I reached the lowest branch and was soon up to Philip.

"Oh, good, Ruth!" he exclaimed. "Now, quick! Burrow up my shirt and pull him out. He's nearly eaten me up."

I burrowed up behind with one hand, and found an excited little ball of fur sharpening its claws on Philip.

It wriggled and squirmed violently as I pulled it out, and almost seemed to turn itself inside out.

"Where shall I put it?" I gasped. "Quick, Philip! I'm going to drop it."

"Put it down your neck!" commanded Philip. "It's all right for you; you've got a vest on. I was bare."

I put it down rather gingerly and then swung down the tree monkeywise, landing with a bump on the ground. The squirrel struggled up and poked his head out at my collar to see what was happening. Philip dropped down beside me and pulled him right out. He took a cookie from his pocket and broke a bit off; the little creature took it between his paws and began nibbling with tiny, sawlike teeth. He kept his eyes fixed on us like two bright points of light; then he went to the pocket and put his head in for more.

We lay on the moss for a long time playing with the squirrel, and he behaved like an inquisitive baby, poking his nose into everything. He ran up our arms and around our necks flicking his bushy tail in our faces. He leaped from Philip's shoulder to mine and tried to nibble my ear. When we teased him by offering him some cookie and snatching it away, he curled up in a ball and sulked.

We put him in Philip's pocket to return him to the nest, but he was an independent squirrel. For Philip was hardly halfway up the tree when his small passenger wriggled out.

"Oh, dear!" exclaimed Philip. "He's escaped, and I'm in an awfully difficult place. He's run right round the other side of the tree and I shall never catch him."

"I don't think you'll have to," I called back from where I stood with my head thrown far back. "I don't think you'll have to catch him; he's going home by himself."

I was right; there was a streak of gray up the trunk, and the little runaway disappeared into his own front door.

"What a clever squirrel!" I cried, dancing about under the tree. "I expect he's snuggled up with his brothers and sisters telling them how he went out with some giants, and I expect his mother is scolding him for not coming back before."

"Perhaps she sent the policeman out, like Aunt Margaret when you ran away," answered Philip, dropping down from a high branch rather suddenly. He rolled over on top of me, and I couldn't be bothered to stop, so we both rolled down to the bottom of the hollow, and lay laughing in the fern.

Chapter 11

MY SHEEP HEAR MY VOICE

PHILIP," I said suddenly, sitting up, "I'm going home now; you see, I specially want to visit somebody on the way back."

"All right," answered Philip contentedly. "We'll go; whom do you want to visit?"

"Mr. Tandy, the shepherd," I replied.

"Good!" agreed Philip. "I like Mr. Tandy; I'll come with you."

I stopped dead, wondering how I could explain. Philip walked on, watching a magpie, unaware of any difficulty.

"Philip," I said, rather awkwardly, "you can't come with me; you see, it's a secret, and I want to see Mr. Tandy alone. It's something you don't know about, and I've got to go by myself."

It was Philip's turn to stop and stare now. He turned

right around and looked as though he thought he had heard wrongly.

"But why?" he asked at last. "You always tell me your secrets. You shouldn't tell Mr. Tandy before me; I'm your brother, and he's an old man."

There was a sort of shadow in his clear blue eyes, and his face was rather pink. I could see he was hurt, and I felt dreadful.

"But you wouldn't understand," I explained desperately. "You see, it's not a make-up or a pretend; it's a real, true, very important secret; you might not believe me and you might laugh."

He looked not only hurt, but downright indignant.

"But I've never laughed before," he said, "and I always believe you. It's very unkind of you, Ruth, to have real true secrets and not tell me. I always tell you mine."

There was a long pause, and I did not know what to say.

"Oh, all right," he said at last, trying to speak casually. "I'll go on home. You'll find me in the orchard when you come."

He turned and went on, and I followed rather miserably. We walked single file in silence as far as the stile where the path divided: one way led over the meadow toward home and one led up to the sheepfolds.

"Good-by," said Philip without looking around. "See you later."

He took the downward path and I took the upward one, but I had not gone many steps before I turned to look back. Philip was walking slowly across the field with his hands in his pockets and his head rather bowed as though he were staring hard at the ground. He must have been very miserable for he was not even watching the sky for birds.

And as I stood staring after his lonely figure, I saw all in a flash—perhaps for the first time—what sort of a brother Philip had been to me. I remembered how gravely he had listened when I used to snuggle my curly head against his shoulder and whisper my baby fancies into his ear. How patiently he had entered into my make-believes with my dolls; how swiftly he would run back from school in case I should be missing him; and how faithfully he had stood by me when I was cross and bad-tempered and punished! As I thought of all these things, I suddenly didn't want to have any secret at all that I could not share with Philip. Of course, I wanted to go on belonging to the Good Shepherd, but not by myself. Philip must belong, too, and then we could enjoy the secret together.

I flew down the hill after him as fast as my legs would carry me, shouting his name at the top of my

voice. He turned round and waited for me, and even as
I ran I could not help thinking how much nicer he was
than I. I would have walked on in a huff and pretended not to hear.

I was quite breathless when I reached him, and sort
of fell against him to stop myself.

"Philip!" I gasped. "I didn't mean it at all. I don't
want to have secrets without you, and I'll tell you
everything always, only you see there's a bit I don't
understand and I can't tell you properly until I've asked
Mr. Tandy; but then I shall know all about it and I'll
tell you in the wigwam tomorrow and then you can
have it, too."

The shadow passed instantly from Philip's eyes, and
his beautiful smile shone out again. There never was a
boy so quick to forgive and forget a quarrel.

"It's all right," he assured me. "I don't mind you
going to tell Mr. Tandy, as long as you tell me afterward. But it will spoil everything if we don't tell each
other our secrets."

I was so pleased to see him happy again that I flung
my arms around his neck and kissed him. I had not
done such a thing for a long time, and he looked a little
breathless and astonished, and glanced around the field
to see that no one was looking. Then he wiped off the
kiss with his sleeve, because it was rather a wet one,

gave me another radiant smile, and trotted off toward home.

I turned and ran back up the hill, but when I had gone halfway up I turned to look at Philip. He was still trotting, but his head was thrown far back; he had forgotten all about everything and was watching swallows.

I was very red in the face when I reached the sheepfolds, because I had climbed the hill so fast. To my great relief Mr. Tandy was there mending the gate, and I ran straight to him and took his great hand in my two small ones.

"Mr. Tandy," I said, without waiting for any introduction, "I've come to tell you something. I've found out all about that story you read me, and I know now that it means me, and that the Good Shepherd means Jesus."

He stood there with his hammer in his hand, looking down at me, with a look of amazing joy on his face.

"I'm real glad to hear it, little maid," he said, rather huskily. "Maybe you'll tell me a bit more about it."

"Oh, yes, I'll tell you about it," I replied, pulling him down beside me on the seat. I was so pleased to find someone who would believe me that I quite forgot to be shy. "I was naughty, and I ran away, and I stayed in a church all night by myself in the dark, and in the

morning the minister found me and took me to his
home. And he showed me a picture of a little lost lamb,
just like yours, Mr. Tandy, and a Shepherd with
wounds in His hands leaning over the precipice; and
the lamb had run away like me, and the Shepherd was
like Jesus, because He came to look for me when He
died for me. So on the way home I asked Him to find
me and to make me good, and now I'm His lamb and I
belong to Him."

Mr. Tandy listened gravely, but his wrinkled old
face was full of happiness.

"Thank God for that, little maid!" he replied. "For if
you belong to Him now, you'll belong to Him forever.
No man can pluck you out of His hand."

"Mr. Tandy," I asked, "are you one of His sheep?"

"Sure, little girl," he answered, "I've been one of
His flock for nearly fifty years."

"Then, Mr. Tandy," I went on eagerly, "have you
ever heard His voice? It says His sheep hear His voice,
but I've listened and listened, and He never says anything to me, and I do want to hear Him."

He thought a long time before answering that question. Then he spoke very slowly.

"I'm going to call my sheep, lassie," he said. "And
when I call, take a look at 'em all, but you specially

mark them ones over by the hedge, and see the difference."

I watched while he gave a low, clear call; every sheep in the meadow lifted its head expectantly and drew a step or two nearer, except for the group by the hedge. They went on feeding quietly as though nothing had happened.

"Why don't they answer?" I asked. "Can't they hear you?"

"They hear me," answered the old man, "but they don't know my voice from all the others because they belonged to another shepherd who took sick; they only joined my flock two days ago. But let 'em walk to the pastures with me for a week or so, and let me fold 'em, and put my hands on their heads, and feed 'em, and they'll soon come to know my voice same as the rest. Now there's many voices speaking to your heart, little girl, and you've only belonged to the Shepherd these few days, so maybe you haven't learned to pick out His voice from all them others—for 'tis a still, small voice."

"Then tell me how I can start," I pleaded.

"Well, 'tis like this," he said at last, after another long pause; "do you ever want to be a bad little lass?"

"Oh, yes, often," I replied. "Before I ran away, I

used to lose my temper and be rude to Aunt Margaret nearly every day."

"Well, then," went on Mr. Tandy, "you mind this: next time you want to lose your temper, you remember there's two voices a-speaking to you. There's the voice of the enemy bidding you kick up a row and stamp your foot and all the rest of it, but if you hold back a minute and listen, maybe you'll hear another voice—a quiet-like voice—bidding you be gentle and do as you're told. That's the voice of the Shepherd. And if you learn to obey that voice, He'll speak again, and you'll find you're hearing Him all the time and everywhere. He talks to me out in these fields, and when I read my Bible He comes to me, and I know it ain't just a Book of black and white print for scholars, but 'tis the voice of my Saviour a-speaking to me."

Drawn by his voice, the sheep had come quite close and were standing near his knees, their mild faces upturned; when he stopped speaking they moved away, cropping the grass.

" 'Twill soon be time for the shearing," observed the old man thoughtfully.

I rose to my feet and held out my hand. "Thank you very much, Mr. Tandy," I said. "I'm going home now to listen, and I hope I shall soon want to get into a temper."

He shook his head. "Don't you wish any such thing!" he warned me. "And don't you try it alone. Remember, it is only the Saviour who can stop you from doing wrong."

He spoke very earnestly, and I thought about it a lot as I ran home across the fields. How queer it was that I couldn't ever stop myself from losing my own temper! Yet I knew I couldn't, because I'd tried.

Philip was not in the orchard, so I went to look for him indoors; rather to my dismay I heard voices in the dining room. They had started tea, and I was late; we were not allowed to be late for tea, so I stepped into the room rather guiltily and made for my seat with an anxious glance at Aunt Margaret. She was looking extremely grim.

"Ruth," she said sharply, "you're late again and I'm not going to have it. Sit down and eat in silence—and you are not to have a chocolate cookie."

Now this was a dreadful punishment, because I loved chocolate cookies and we hardly ever had them. I gave a little stamp with my foot and threw back my head. All my happiness disappeared and a great torrent of angry words seemed to come springing up out of my heart all ready to tumble out of my mouth. In fact, I had actually opened my mouth, when I suddenly remembered!

If I got in a rage now I shouldn't be able to listen to the quiet voice of the Good Shepherd; and if I didn't listen now perhaps He wouldn't speak to me again.

It was so difficult to stop those angry words that I had to clap my hand in front of my mouth to keep them in. And so I stood in the middle of the room, listening, while my aunt and Philip stared at me in the greatest astonishment.

"What is the matter?" asked my aunt, coldly. "Have you bitten your tongue?"

I didn't answer, because it had suddenly come back to me—the verse that Mr. Tandy and I had been talking about—"My sheep hear my voice, and I know them, and they follow me." Following the Shepherd meant being like Him: if I was going to be like Him I must stop stamping, shouting, answering back and sulking, because the Lord had never done any of these things. "Help me to follow You," I whispered in my heart; "stop me being angry, quick."

I drew a great big breath and put my hand back in my pocket. I sat down in my chair without saying anything, for my anger was all going away. Auntie still continued to stare at me, as though she was rather scared as to what might happen next, but I went on munching my bread and butter in silence. I did not look at the chocolate cookies, because I was afraid the sight of them might make me angry again.

We were all very quiet for the rest of tea, and when it was finished Aunt Margaret said that, as it was my first day up after my cold, I had better go straight to bed. I did not mind at all, for I had such a lot to think about that I wanted to be alone. I got in as soon as possible, and lay by my open window staring out at the summer night and growing darkness.

The sky was the color of deep harebells, and when I'd stared at it a long time I suddenly discovered that there were stars hidden in its blue depths; a few late birds twittered goodnight to each other in the damson plum trees, and the quiet air smelled of lilac. I lay with my arms thrown above my head on the pillow, looking and listening, till I fell asleep. I was perfectly happy, because two beautiful things had happened that day for the very first time. I had heard the voice of the Good Shepherd, and I had swarmed a tree.

Chapter 12

THE ACCIDENT

WE MEANT TO GO straight to the wigwam next day, and talk about the secret, but just as we climbed over the stile Terry popped up out of the ditch like a rabbit and said he'd come to spend the morning with us. He had hidden in the ditch to give us a surprise, so having been duly surprised we all settled down on the bank to make plans.

As a matter of fact Terry had already made all the plans. We were merely meant to follow them. He had found a high ash tree with a wood pigeon's nest at the top, and if Philip wanted to see a wood pigeon's egg he'd better come along right now because there were two beauties. It was an ash tree with a fork; Terry's plan was to collect some branches and bits of wood and make a sort of platform opposite where we could sit and watch the eggs hatch. The mother pigeon would probably think we were some other big birds making a

nest like hers, and not mind at all—at least, so Terry
said. Terry always seemed to know exactly what birds
were thinking.

We were thrilled with the idea, and went off single
file through the wood; the tree in question was quite a
long way off, across the stream in the valley, and some
way in among the larches that grew on the farther side.
These trees were beautiful by now, studded all over
with crimson baby cones, like jewels on a coronet, the
sweeping boughs such a vivid green that other trees
looked dull in comparison. When I was tiny I always
imagined that the fairies swung on the pine boughs, but
now I knew better. I still loved them, and I lingered
behind for a moment to finger the tassels while the
boys went crashing on ahead. The tree was well off the
beaten track, and the brambles and nettles grew thick. I
followed in their path as best I could, but even so my
bare legs got dreadfully scratched, and were the color
of unripe blackberries when I finally caught up. I sat
down on the tree root and began mopping up the
scratches with my handkerchief.

"Sorry," said Philip, apologetically. "I forgot your
legs were shorter than ours for jumping. You keep up
on the way home and I'll tread the brambles down for
you."

Terry stared at my damaged knees. "She's a game

little kid, ain't she?" he observed, and I felt as though I'd been awarded. I would willingly have walked through brambles and nettles to have earned such praise.

Terry had no time to waste; he crouched like a small panther and then leaped for the nearest bough of the ash. He caught hold with one hand and dragged himself up, the muscles rippling all over his taut body. I have never since met a child of eleven years quite so strong and lithe as Terry.

"Now," he yelled, lying astride the bough, "hoist up Ruth, and I'll catch hold!" Philip heaved me up on his shoulders, and Terry seized my wrists and pulled until I was able to clutch the bough; I gave a convulsive wriggle, more or less turned myself inside out, and arrived panting beside Terry. Philip gave two mighty leaps, but fell backwards. On the third he caught hold of the branch and dragged himself up too. So we sat dangling our legs, like three happy monkeys, and shared our lunch with Terry, who always took it for granted that my aunt included him in the housekeeping, and always ate much more than his share. But we gave it ungrudgingly, for we had long ago decided that Terry's mother must have starved him at home, as no one but a starving child could eat so wolfishly.

"Come on," said Terry, gulping down the last mouthful, "we'll nip up and take a look at her."

Off he went like a sailor on a rope, while Philip and I followed more slowly. The nest was on a sort of platform of interwoven twigs, and as we got nearer to it we could hear the nervous murmur of the pigeon deep in her throat. Suddenly there was a whirr of beautiful pearl-grey wings and the bird rose and settled on the very topmost twig of the opposite fork, where she sat looking down at us and her nest.

It was such a careless nest that I wondered how the oblong eggs escaped rolling out; just a few loosely woven sticks with some moss stuffed in the holes. But the eggs were burning hot and well cared for, and the mother was in a frenzy of anxiety. Terry leaned back and stared at her.

"Nice spot to watch them eggs from," he remarked coolly. "I'm a-going up there myself."

"You couldn't!" protested Philip. "The branches wouldn't bear you; why they'll hardly bear the pigeon."

But Terry was rather a boastful little boy. If anyone ever said "you couldn't do" a thing, he immediately had to do it to show that he could. So now he merely said, "I'll show you," and swung himself across to the opposite fork.

Philip and I watched in fascinated silence, as the

thin, agile little figure mounted higher and higher. The pigeon saw him coming, rose softly, and alighted back with half-spread wings on to her nest. We had no eye for anyone but Terry. We had seen him do such daring and almost impossible feats before, but this beat all. Already the gray stems were bending outwards beneath his weight.

"Stop!" called Philip, in a rather husky voice; but Terry took no notice; instead, his gay laugh came ringing back to us through the leaves, and still he climbed—only he was climbing very cautiously now.

"He's got there!" breathed Philip. Indeed he had. He was standing out right against the sky, clinging to a frail branch. The wind that moved lazily over the treetops had caught his hair and blown it back from his face, and his dark starry eyes were alight with laughter and triumph. When I think of Terry, that is how I like to remember him, because it was the last time that we, or anyone else, ever saw him well and strong.

I can hardly mention what happened next. Philip and I have never spoken of it to each other, and indeed I know that we both try never to think of it, although I shall remember it all my life. Terry, ignoring our frightened pleadings, began to swing to and fro; twice the branch bowed with him, but the third time it snapped. Terry was flung outward into space.

He gave one shrill scream that shattered the silence of the summer woods, and haunted me in the night for many weeks. Then we heard his light body crashing through the leaves and twigs, which mercifully partly broke his fall; then came a sickening thud—and silence.

I don't know to this day how Philip and I escaped falling after him and breaking our necks—we swung down that tree at such a speed. Even so, Philip reached the bottom long before I did, but I got there somehow, and dropped to the ground gasping and sobbing. I lay in a trembling heap with my face hidden in the moss. I dared not look at Terry.

Philip was down on his knees beside him, and had come to the conclusion that Terry was still breathing. He came over to me at last and put his arm around me.

"Ruth," he said, in a voice that was shaky and fearful, "I'm not quite sure, but I think he's alive. We can't possibly carry him; we shall have to fetch some men and a doctor. I think I'd better go, because I can run faster than you and I'm not crying so much. But, Ruth, we can't leave him alone, because he might wake up and be frightened and want someone. Would you mind staying with him, and I'll come back as quick as I can?"

I shuddered and shook my head violently; I couldn't be left alone—I was much too frightened. I clung to

Philip sobbing, and begged him to let me go instead; but he wouldn't hear of it.

"You see, Ruth," he explained quickly, "he may die very soon, and if the doctor came in time he may be able to do something to make him better. I shall get there much quicker because of my legs being so much longer. You must let me go, and try and be brave and stop crying."

He freed himself from my grasp, gently enough, and made off like the wind. I lay and listened to his footsteps crackling over the dead leaves and twigs, until the sound died away and only the murmuring of the pigeons broke the silence of the woods.

Now that I was left alone it occurred to me that I must make myself look at Terry. So I clenched my teeth and my fists, and sat up.

What I actually saw was a great relief to me. I had never seen anyone badly hurt or unconscious before. I had imagined that it would be a very horrid sight; but Terry, lying on his back with his arms spread wide, might have been asleep, except that his lips were unnaturally pale, and he breathed so lightly. He did not look hurt or frightened—only curiously peaceful, and as I sat there staring at him I began to feel curiously peaceful myself—as though he must soon wake up refreshed by such deep sleep and we should all be happy again.

The minutes seemed like hours and Terry did not stir; still I sat watching and wondering. Perhaps Terry was already dead—the thought made me feel cold and sick. Once again my eyes filled with frightened tears. If only Philip would come back! What was death, and if Terry were dead, where had he gone? We should bury his quiet little body under the ground, but I knew that that was not really Terry—Terry, I supposed, had gone to heaven, like we sang about in hymns in church; but would Terry be happy? One grubby, rather naughty little boy, among all those golden streets and white wings!

Then I suddenly remembered Jane Collins, who had gone "to be with the Lord"—and the radiant face of the child in my dream. Perhaps dying just meant going to live with the Shepherd—hearing Him speak with our proper ears and seeing Him with real eyes, instead of just inside our hearts—that would be lovely, I thought. No wonder the little girl had looked so happy; and perhaps that was why Terry looked so peaceful.

But Terry did not know about the Good Shepherd, so he could not go to live with Him. I was sure Terry had never heard anything about it; if only I'd had a chance to tell him! If he didn't die I should tell him at once, and then Philip and he and I would all belong together. After all, it wasn't Terry's fault that he had never asked to be found and forgiven—it was really mine, because I had kept the secret to myself.

So I sat hugging my knees, with my eyes fixed on Terry's still face, torn between hope and fear. Every few minutes I thought I heard Philip coming, but each time it turned out to be only a rabbit, or a bird, or a gust of wind in the trees. The sunshine streamed through the thin foliage of the pines and rested in a bright patch on Terry's hair; almost as though God were touching him, I thought to myself. I remembered how in the Gospel of Luke, which I read every morning, the Saviour had touched men and women and children who were hurt and ill, and they always got well at once.

"O God," I whispered, looking up through the branches, "please make Terry better—don't let him die—we want him here so much. Amen."

It was then that I heard Philip's voice through the trees, and men's voices talking, too. A moment later a procession came into sight with Philip leading the way; behind him came Uncle Peter, who was always at home on Saturday, and kind Doctor Paterson who had come to see me when I had measles; behind them came two men in dark uniforms carrying a stretcher; these were the ambulance men.

Dr. Paterson knelt down at once and put his fingers

on Terry's brown wrist; he held it for a long time and then passed his hands over Terry's head, drew back his eyelids, and bent his legs and arms backward and forward very gently. Then he turned to me:

"Has the boy moved since he fell?" he asked.

"No," I answered, "He's been as though he was fast asleep all the time." Then, emboldened by the sound of my own voice, I gave his coat a little tug; "Is he dead?" I whispered.

Dr. Paterson put his arm round my shoulder. "No," he answered gently, "he's not dead, but he's very badly hurt; you were a good girl to stay here alone and look after him; now we'll take him to the hospital as soon as we can, and I'm going to see what I can do for him."

Very gently and carefully Terry was lifted on to the stretcher, and the men set off through the brambles with the precious burden between them. Uncle Peter, seeing how white and scared I looked, stooped down and picked me up in his arms like a baby; I snuggled up against him, and laid my throbbing head on his shoulder, and felt greatly comforted. I had always been good friends with Uncle Peter.

But I noticed Philip's face only when he glanced toward me, for he had walked with his head turned sideways; he said nothing, but his lips were pressed tightly together and his eyes were desperate—they re-

minded me of the eyes of a rabbit I had once found
caught in a trap. His cheeks high up were scarlet, but
the rest of his face was quite white; in that moment I
realized that all my uncertain fears were nothing to
Philip's steady misery. I longed to run and comfort
him, but knew that there was nothing I could say or do;
nothing would comfort him except Terry's getting
well.

We all walked very slowly so as not to jolt the
stretcher, for the ground was rough and uneven. We
took a narrow, overgrown path which led on to the
road, and the hazel bushes brushed my face as I lay in
Uncle Peter's arms; the ambulance was waiting there,
and Dr. Paterson climbed in with Terry while the men
sat in front.

"When will you tell us if he's better?" I asked, just
as he was about to shut the door.

"I shall be passing your house tomorrow," said the
doctor, "and I'll drop in and let you know."

The door was shut and the engine started up; the
ambulance sped off in a cloud of white dust. Uncle
Peter, Philip and I were left to trudge home. Uncle
asked us a few questions about Terry on the way, but
otherwise we were very silent; nobody felt like talking.

It was a long, wretched day; we hung about the
garden unable to settle down to anything, and with no

appetite for our meals. Aunt Margaret felt sorry for us and read aloud to us in the evening, but we were both glad when bedtime arrived. She came upstairs and kissed us good night, but as soon as her footsteps had died away I hopped out of bed and ran over to Philip. He was lying huddled up in bed, and I think he had been crying, for his voice sounded sniffy and his pillow was damp. I got under the quilt at the bottom and curled myself up in a ball like a kitten.

"Ruth," whispered Philip, rather shakily, "do you think he'll die?"

"No," I answered decidedly, "I don't."

"Why not?" inquired Philip, rather surprised at my being so sure of myself. "Did Dr. Paterson say anything to you when I wasn't listening?"

I wriggled my bare toes up and down under the quilt, like I always did when I was shy. It was difficult to explain, but I thought now was the moment to try and tell.

"Well, you see," I answered, "when you'd gone to get the others, I prayed to God very hard that Terry would get better again, so I expect he will."

Philip stared at me over the top of the sheet.

"So did I," he admitted, slowly. "I said, 'O God, please don't let Terry die,' all the way home, but I don't know whether it was much use; I'm not a very good boy and I usually forget to say my prayers, and nothing much happens when I do."

"But Philip," I said, uncurling myself, and sitting up straight, because I was so very much in earnest, "you don't have to be a specially good person to say your prayers; you just have to belong to the Shepherd. That's what my secret was, that I was going to tell you about today. I didn't make it up; the minister told me when I ran away, and it's in the Bible, too. When we're naughty we're like sheep that run away and get lost, and can't find the way back. But Jesus is the Shepherd; He comes to look for us, and when we ask Him, He finds us—but He always waits till we ask. Then we belong to Him and He listens to everything we say, and He speaks to us and tells us how to be good. Mr. Tandy told me that, and He spoke to me last night and stopped me from losing my temper with Aunt Margaret, when she wouldn't let me have a chocolate cookie."

I could see Philip staring at me, his face pale in the moonlight. "Go on," he said, "and stop wriggling your toes."

"There's not much more to say," I continued, "except that when Terry was lying on the ground the sun suddenly shone through the trees right on his hair, and I thought perhaps it was God's way of touching him

and making him better, like Jesus touched people in
the Bible. And after that I was almost sure he wasn't
going to die."

There was a long silence, broken at last by Philip.

"Did you ask Him to find you?" he asked, curiously.

I nodded. "I did it on the way home," I said, "in the
primrose woods, under a tree. I asked Him to forgive
me for being naughty, and to find me and make me one
of His lambs as the minister said—and oh, Philip, I
wish you would come with me and see that minister,
because he'd tell you about it much better than me, and
I do so want you to belong to the Shepherd, too."

"I wish I did," said Philip in a sober voice. "Do you
think I could?"

"I'm sure you could," I answered, very decidedly. "I
should think you'd be much easier to find than me
because you're so much better—I don't think you'd
take much finding at all."

But Philip shook his head. "You don't know," he
said sadly. "You only see me outside. I'm not at all
good inside."

"Well," I argued, "it doesn't matter. I'll show you
my picture and you'll see; the sheep there is nearly
falling over a precipice, he's got so lost, but the Shepherd is just going to find him all the same."

I tiptoed across the passage and returned with my

precious picture in my hand. We both went over to the window, and could see it quite clearly because the full moon was shining right in at the window. Philip went on looking at it for a long time.

"Could I ask now, Ruth?" he said at last, rather anxiously.

I nodded.

"Then you must go away," he explained, "because I shall have to be alone—we'll talk more about it in the morning."

So I left him, with his elbows on the window sill, looking at the hills. I snuggled into my bed and stared up sleepily at the millions of stars, and thought of my story.

"There is joy in the presence of the angels of God over one sinner that repenteth"—that was how the story ended. Everybody was a sinner, so I supposed Philip was, too; but he was being found, so perhaps up above the stars all the angels of God were singing and being joyful over Philip—and a little girl on earth was sharing their joy.

Chapter 13

A VISIT TO THE PARSONAGE

THE HOLIDAYS PASSED all too quickly because there was so much to do. The doctor came to see us next day, and as soon as we heard his car stop we flung ourselves out of the gate, and nearly knocked him backward in our eagerness to hear the news.

"Steady, steady!" exclaimed Dr. Paterson, collaring us both. "If you knock me out I shall not be able to tell you anything."

Terry was alive, he told us, but he had hurt his back and head very badly indeed, and would be in the hospital many weeks. His mother was with him nearly all the time now, but as soon as he was a little better he would probably be moved to another hospital—a special hospital for people with broken bones. We could not go and visit him because it was too far away, but we would probably be able to write to him in a few weeks' time.

This was quite enough to calm our fears and make us

happy again. Terry was alive and being looked after; he would certainly get better soon, we told ourselves, just as we had always got better in time from measles and colds and tummy-aches. So we stopped worrying, and settled down to enjoy the last few days of our holidays as much as we could.

We decided that we must pay one last visit to each of our friends, so Philip went to call on the birdman, and was taken down to see a moorhen's nest, and I paid a visit to Mr. Tandy in the sheepfolds. But there wasn't much time for conversation, because Mr. Tandy was busy shearing the sheep.

The last day of all we set apart for visiting the minister, and we set out about half-past three, because I'm afraid we thought it would be rather nice to arrive about time to eat; and as we walked along the road we talked about our secret. I couldn't help remembering the last time I walked along that same road! How hot and angry and miserable I had been then—how happy I was now! The secret had certainly made a great difference.

"I don't suppose it's made such a difference to you," I observed to Philip, "because you weren't so naughty as me, and things didn't make you angry." Philip picked a dandelion clock and thoughtfully blew it to pieces.

"It has made a great difference," he answered slow-

ly, "because now I feel as if I had found something I
was looking for—you see, I'd really been wanting it for
a long time."

"Had you?" I asked, surprised. "I didn't think you
knew anything about it! You never told me."

"Well, I didn't think you'd understand," he explained. "And anyhow I wasn't really sure what I did
want. One day, a long time ago, I was in the woods
by myself; you were at home because you'd been
naughty—and I found a little newly hatched sparrow
lying on the ground, nearly dead. He was giving some
little chirps, but his body was getting cold and he
couldn't have lived long. He had fallen out of the nest,
and I tried and tried to put him back, but it was just too
high, because I was only a little boy then; so I kneeled
down with the baby sparrow in my hands, and prayed
for someone tall to come and put it back for me; and
just when I was saying Amen, Jake from Edward's
farm came down the path to haul firewood, and put it
back as easy as anything.

"So, I thought, God must mind about baby sparrows,
and I thought about it quite a lot. Then, the next
Sunday in church we read some texts about God knowing when sparrows fell out of their nests, and I listened
extra carefully. The preacher said that we were much
more valuable to God than sparrows, and that, if we

belonged to Him, He took care of us and loved us specially. I can't remember it very well, but somehow I wished I could belong to Him, only I didn't know how to begin. And ever since then, when things have gone wrong, I've wished I knew more, and I've been miserable. Then when you showed me your picture, and told me about being found and forgiven, I knew that I'd discovered about the beginning. Now I feel happy, because I know that Jesus loves me and will look after me, just like the sparrow that fell out of his nest."

It was a very long speech for Philip; he went rather pink at the end of it, and buried his face in the hedge, pretending to look for a nest that wasn't there. I skipped happily on up the hill thinking what a lovely secret ours was because there were so many new things to learn about it—to me He was the Shepherd who carried lambs, while to Philip He was the God who looked after the sparrows. But it was all the same really, because the lamb was lost and found, and the sparrow had fallen and was picked up.

The village lay at the bottom of the hill, and we marched in at the parsonage gate very sure of a welcome. We did not have to walk far, for my friend was in his shirt sleeves mowing the lawn, and recognized me at once. He seemed delighted to see us both. He did not even ask us if we would stay to tea; he simply said,

"You've both arrived just at the right moment." It
certainly seemed as though we had, for no sooner had I
introduced Philip, than Mrs. Robinson, the minister's
wife, appeared on the lawn with a tray. From the way
Mr. Robinson rushed indoors and fetched jam tarts and
chocolate spread, you might almost have thought that
we were expected!

We had a lovely time. Mr. and Mrs. Robinson sat in
deck-chairs and we sat on a rug and ate a lot because
Mrs. Robinson assured us that jam tarts and chocolate
spread were not rationed. Mrs. Robinson was quite
young, with pretty hair and eyes that laughed, and I
thought privately that I should like her to be my mother. But I discovered later that she was already mother
of some twins, asleep in a baby carriage under a beech
tree, and if we could stay till a quarter to six, I could
see them bathed.

I assured her that we could easily stay till then because Auntie had said we needn't be home till supper at
seven, and it only took us half an hour if we hurried. So
she said she would call me when she was ready, and
went indoors with the empty tray while Philip and I
turned eager and rather jammy faces to Mr. Robinson.

"You tell, Philip," I began.

"No, you!" said my brother, "You did it first."

"Oh, all right," I agreed. "We've got a secret to tell

you, Mr. Robinson—we both belong to the Shepherd now: we've both asked Him to find us and forgive us for being naughty, and we're both awfully happy."

Just for a moment, Mr. Robinson's face reminded me of Mr. Tandy's when I had first told him about my secret—although they were not in the least alike really. Only they both looked so joyful. He leaned forward in his chair.

"Tell me all about it," he said.

So we told him all about it; I knelt upright, and Philip lay on the grass with his face cupped in his hands and his eyes fixed on Mr. Robinson. After we had said a great deal, he started talking to us in his quiet, kind voice. He talked mostly about reading our Bibles.

"You must think about your Bibles as though they were the Shepherd's Book of rules," he said. "Pick out a special verse every day and remember that it is a message to you straight from God. If it tells you to be thoughtful or to work hard, or to love other people, then ask Him to make you able to do it. If it's something God promises to do for you, ask Him to make His promise come true to you; and if it's a story, try to think what lesson it's meant to teach you. Hold on to it all day long; you will learn a little more about following the Shepherd, and listening to His voice every day."

"We'll do it together," I said, eagerly; "what fun we shall have choosing the verses!"

"Yes," answered Philip. "I suppose we shall; but how shall we know what to read? The Bible's a big Book and it's not all very interesting—at least not to children, is it?"

"No," answered Mr. Robinson, "there are parts of the Bible that you will learn to love and understand only when you are much older but all the same there is a great deal that children can understand, too; before you go home I'll give you each a card. On it is written down what you must read every day; then you will be quite all right, because every reading on that card is suitable for children—and I will give you each a little book that explains the difficult parts and helps you."

Chapter 14

I BATHE THE TWINS AND LOSE MY TEMPER

I WAS JUST OPENING my mouth to say "Thank you" when Mrs. Robinson appeared at the window, wearing an apron. "Twins' bedtime, Ruth," she called. "Do you want to come and watch?" I jumped up. "Will you excuse me, please, Mr. Robinson?" I inquired, a little anxiously, for I did not wish him to think me rude.

"Certainly," he replied. "You go and help Mother: she'll be glad of a nursemaid; Philip and I will stay here a little longer, and do some more talking."

I sped across the lawn, and into the house. The twins were crawling about on the carpet while their mother collected their night things. They were ten months old and very lively, and I, who had never had anything to do with babies, thought I had never seen anything to equal them.

I spent a glorious half-hour. Once they were safely in

the big bath, Mrs. Robinson let me soap their plump
little bodies and then pour the water all over them;
then we sailed a yellow sponge duck, and the twins
screamed with laughter and beat the water with their
fat little hands. I was allowed to sprinkle them with
sweet smelling powder, and when they were safely in
their nightgowns I was given a soft little hairbrush
with which I brushed their hair up on end. It was not
proper hair at all; it was more like yellow chicken-
down that rolled itself into sausage-curls down the middle of their heads; and all the time I was doing it they
wriggled, and chuckled, and tried to bite their toes.

It was not till their mother was tucking them firmly
into their cots that I noticed the picture that hung on
the wall behind them; it was another picture of the
Good Shepherd—but it was different from mine. This
Shepherd was standing by a lake, with His hand
stretched out to bless the little lambs that stood beside
Him and lay asleep at His feet.

It was an evening picture, and it reminded me of the
lambs in Mr. Tandy's sheepfold, when the sun sank
behind the woods and the shadows crept up the fields.

"Why," I cried joyfully, pointing up at it. "I've got a
Good Shepherd picture, too, but it's not like that—my
sheep is on a precipice."

"I know your picture," answered Mrs. Robinson,

"and I love it very much. Later I shall show it to the twins; but they are not old enough to understand anything about precipices yet. I like to think that all through the night, when I'm asleep, the Good Shepherd is looking after my babies for me; so I put that picture there to remind me, and whenever I look at it I remember they are perfectly safe."

I stared at the twins. They had both fallen asleep instantly; Janet had curled herself up and had stuffed two fingers into her mouth; Robin lay on his back with his arms thrown out on the pillow, his cheeks flushed with the warmth of sudden, deep sleep. They lay so still and breathed so lightly that I could almost imagine that they had been hushed to rest by the outstretched hand of the Good Shepherd.

I nestled up to Mrs. Robinson and looked up into her face. "Can I come again?" I whispered.

"Of course you can," she replied. "You can come on Saturday, a week from now, if your aunt will let you—I'll write and ask her. I expect you have a holiday on Saturday. We'll take them out, and then you shall help me give them their supper and put them to bed. It's a great treat for me to have a nurse, and I can see that you're handy with babies."

I blushed with pride and slipped my hand into hers. I couldn't exactly have Mrs. Robinson for my mother, but perhaps in time I might become a sort of older sister to the twins.

On returning to the garden I found Mr. Robinson and Philip in conversation. I was eager to get back and ask my aunt about that Saturday, and my delight was doubled when the minister said that Philip might come too, and help him in the garden. We'd all have something to eat together. Saturday afternoon was Mr. Robinson's weekly holiday and we should always find him at home.

We got back in good time for our supper, and I ran straight to my aunt.

"Auntie," I cried, hopping about on one foot, "Mrs. Robinson has invited me to tea with her on next Saturday—her and the babies—and I can push the carriage and put them to bed. I can go, can't I? Do say Yes!"

My aunt looked rather annoyed.

"Who is this Mrs. Robinson, Ruth?" she asked, rather coldly. "You are not to visit people without consulting me; I have never heard of the lady."

"Oh, she's quite all right, Auntie," I assured her, anxiously. "She's a very nice lady indeed, a minister's wife at Fairways; she's going to write to you."

"I should hope so," retorted my aunt, "but I'm afraid the answer will have to be No this time. Miss Montgomery called this afternoon to say that her little niece was coming to stay, and I said that you would go and play with her that afternoon. I'm sorry you should be disappointed, but perhaps this Mrs. Robinson will invite you another day. If she is really the wife of the minister of Fairways, I have no objection to your accepting; I have heard they are very nice people."

I flew into a rage at once.

"But Auntie," I stormed, "you know that I *hate* going to tea with Miss Montgomery; and I *hate* Juliana Montgomery—she's like a little white mouse. She doesn't know how to play anything nice, and we have to sit indoors and play dominoes, and I *hate* dominoes. Oh, *please*, Auntie, say I needn't go—I told Mrs. Robinson I could come!"

"Then you had no business to tell Mrs. Robinson," replied my aunt, sharply. "I never heard such nonsense! You are never to accept invitations without my permission—and stand still while you talk; you are making me quite dizzy."

But I had thoroughly lost my temper by this time, and was nearly crying with disappointment.

"I won't go!" I shouted. "I shall go where I like—I told Mrs. Robinson I'd come, and I shall go, and you shan't stop me!"

My aunt took hold of my arm.

"Go straight to bed," she said, firmly. "Don't let me

hear any more of this rudeness; I thought you were
going to try and improve, but this does not look like
improvement at all—off you go!"

I shook myself free and marched off with my head in
the air.

"I don't care," I muttered over my shoulder—and
slammed the door behind me as hard as I could.

But I *did* care—very much indeed! Almost before
I'd reached the top of the stairs, I'd realized what I'd
done, and by the time I crept into bed I thought my
heart was breaking. I curled up in a ball, buried my
face in the pillow, and wept and wept.

I had forgotten to listen to the voice of the Good
Shepherd. Perhaps He would never speak to me again;
perhaps He would stop loving me. Perhaps I should
even stop belonging to Him, and then there would be
no one to help me to be good. Oh, why hadn't I waited
and listened?

"Ruth, what *is* the matter? You mustn't cry like
this!"

I had been sobbing so bitterly that I never heard my
aunt come in. I turned around quickly and swallowed
my tears, for I did not really want her to see how sorry
I was. She was sitting by my bed, and she had a glass of
milk and a plate of cookies in her hand.

"What is the matter, Ruth?" she asked again, and

her voice was rather anxious, for she had never seen me cry like that before.

I tried to answer in my ordinary voice, but could not. I buried my head in the pillow and began crying again.

I did not want to tell her, but it suddenly occurred to me that she might be able to answer my questions, and I wanted to know the answer so badly that I blurted it all out.

"It's the Shepherd," I sobbed. "I lost my temper and perhaps I shan't belong to Him any more. Oh, Auntie, do you think I shall be able to come back to Him, if I'm good next time?"

I lifted my face in my eagerness to hear her answer, but she was staring at me as if I had lost my senses.

"What *are* you talking about, Ruth?" she asked, helplessly.

I dived for the chair and found my picture in my Bible: I pulled it out, and held it in front of her with a great sniff and a gulp.

"That," I answered. "You see I was His sheep, but I forgot to listen, and perhaps He'll never speak to me again, because I lost my temper so badly. Do you think, Auntie, He'd forgive me just this once?"

My aunt was staring very hard at the picture, and she didn't speak for a long time.

"Who gave you this picture, Ruth?" she asked at last.

"Mr. Robinson," I replied, "and he told me all about it—you know the story, don't you, Auntie? Do you think He will, Auntie, if I never, never do it again?"

She was still staring at the picture and the answer was a long time in coming.

"Auntie," I whispered impatiently, giving her arm a little shake, "do you think He might?"

"If you are really sorry for being naughty, and are determined to try and be different, I am quite sure God will forgive you. You had better ask Him."

Her voice was gentle, and very sad. We were silent again for a time.

"You do know the story, don't you, Auntie?" I asked, timidly; something on her face made me feel rather uncertain.

"Oh, yes," she answered, "but I used to know it much better than I do now. Still, I'm glad it's been a help to you, and I wish I could have taught you more myself. You must go and see this minister again and have him tell you more."

I was about to remark that it might be a good idea if I went to see him instead of going to tea with Miss Montgomery, but I thought better of it. After all, I couldn't really be sorry, and have my own way as well.

So I blew my nose very hard instead, and settled down to my milk and cookies.

My aunt stayed with me while I ate, but we said very little. When I had finished, she kissed me good night and left me very drowsy and quite comforted. Before I fell asleep I buried my face in the pillow again, and breathed out a prayer for forgiveness to the One who stood close beside me, and who cared equally for lost lambs, fallen sparrows, sleeping babies, and naughty little girls.

Chapter 15

WE GET A LETTER

THE SUMMER TERM sped by. Philip went wild over cricket and we spent long happy evenings bowling over to each other. Philip's school was a good way off and he had no friends from our district. I never wanted to have anything to do with girls when Philip was about.

The baby birds we had watched and loved were all fledged and out in the world by now, and the nests deserted. Early in the mornings we often climbed the hills to watch the larks spring up from the fern and soar singing up into the sunrise. We loved to lie silently on the hill when the sky was a blaze of dawn; we watched the mists scatter across the plain and the brightness give way to clear blue. Then we would race home to breakfast, leaping over the rocks and bushes, shouting to each other as we ran, so that the mountain

154

sheep fled away from in front of us while the ravine between the hills echoed with the sound of our voices.

The summer holidays had come around again before we heard from Terry. All the summer he had been in a children's hospital, and from time to time we got news of him from Dr. Paterson. We wrote to him quite a lot and told him all about the woods, what flowers were coming out, and what birds we had seen but he never answered. So it was a great surprise when the postman, meeting us at the gate one morning, handed us a letter addressed to us.

Nobody but Father or Mother ever wrote to us, and this was certainly not their writing. It was larger, and shaky, and looked as though the writer was not very used to writing letters. Philip politely handed it to me to open and looked over my shoulder while I read.

"Dear Filip and Ruth," it said, "I am come home but i has to stay in bed. Please come to see me from Terry my adress is Willow Cottage, The Hollow, Tanglewoods."

We were so impatient to start that we could scarcely eat our dinner, and we talked about it all the time. My aunt seemed slightly doubtful when we showed her the note, but said we could go all the same.

"I only hope it's a clean cottage, and that you won't catch anything. Don't stay too long, will you?"

Dinner over we raced to our rooms for we each wanted to take Terry a present. I found a bar of chocolate and Philip found a catapult, so we wrapped them up in separate parcels and put them in our pockets. Then we hurled ourselves out of the front door and set off for Tanglewoods. Tanglewoods was such a little village that it was really quite difficult to tell when you got there. There was a house called the Goat and Compasses. A long way farther down the road was a shop which sold groceries and candles and cattlefood and medicine and cough-mixtures, and had a post office in one corner. Farther on still was a tiny church with some old tombstones falling backward. But none of these by themselves could be called the village, for the real Tanglewoods consisted of scattered farms and cottages resting on the sides of the low hills, and of barns and outhouses hidden among the hopyards. No one knew where Tanglewoods started, and no one knew where it ended. Terry's address took us some time to trace.

We came through the woods, and down over the ridge where hay from the late second mowing lay in tidy rows up the meadows. The view in front reminded us of a patchwork quilt, with its dark green hopyards, golden corn-fields ripe for the sickle. Everywhere we looked we saw risings and hollows and little hills and valleys, and we stood for a while trying to guess in which particular hollow Terry lived.

There was no one in sight, and we made for the nearest farm to ask the way. We found a woman churning in a cool stone dairy. She came to the door, and pointed farther down the valley.

"You'll be meaning that tumbledown place down Sheep's Hollow; there's a gypsy sort of woman lives there with a boy—she's been up begging a deal of times. Follow the track down through the bushes, and then follow the brook—it leads right down into the hollow."

We thanked her and passed on, and she stood staring after us curiously as though she would have liked to have know our business at Willow Cottage. But we did not want to be hindered, and we hurried down the hill as fast as we could until we could see the cottage just below us, with its broken chimney and the holes in the roof where slates had blown off.

It was a dark little hollow that had once been part of a quarry, although the clematis vine had covered up the bare rocks and made a green curtain round its sides. The stream trickled through it in a stagnant, slimy ooze, and we wondered why anyone should have chosen to build a cottage in such a damp, cheerless spot. But we learned later from Terry that it had been built as a hut for storing dynamite for the quarry, and only later made into a house.

It looked so desolate and deserted, with its broken windows stuffed with rag that we hung back half-frightened. Surely Terry couldn't live here! But even as we stood hesitating at the entrance of the hollow, the door opened and a woman appeared and stood staring back at us.

We knew that she was Terry's mother because of her great black eyes, but even so we felt afraid of her. She was a big, powerful woman with dark skin and black, untidy hair gathered back in a handkerchief. Her face was hard and unhappy and she looked at us as if she disliked us.

Nobody spoke for a moment or two—then the woman broke the silence.

"Well," she asked, "what be you kids a-wanting here?"

"Please," explained Philip, "Terry wrote us a letter to come and see him, so we came. Please, we're so glad that he's well enough to come home."

The woman's face did not clear.

"Be you the children as was with my Terry when he fell?" she asked, suspiciously.

"Yes," we answered, rather guiltily.

"You didn't ought to have let him done it," she

muttered. "Still, he's been carrying on something awful about you two coming to see 'im, so you'd best come in."

She jerked the door back roughly and led the way inside. We followed, but I slipped my hand into Philip's and held it tight. The little room into which she entered was gloomy, hot, and airless, and there was a queer smell, too, that made me want to sneeze. There was only one little window, and it was too high to see through it.

A moment later we had forgotten all this, and had both run forward with a cry of welcome. For on the bed in the corner lay Terry, and we had not seen him for three-and-a-half months.

Of course we knew it was Terry because we were expecting him; but otherwise I'm not sure that we should have recognized him. He was so changed; his face had lost its color and seemed much smaller, and his great unhappy eyes seemed to have grown much larger. His arms that were once so brown and strong were as weak and small as little white sticks, and the sight of him lying there brought a lump into my throat, so that at first I could not speak.

He did not smile at us, for his face had grown so sullen and unhappy that he looked as though he hardly knew how to smile. He held out his hand and remarked gravely that he was real pleased to see us, and he'd been looking out for us ever since morning.

We said equally gravely that we were very pleased to see him, and then there was a long silence because none of us could think of anything to say at all.

Philip broke it at last by inquiring how Terry had enjoyed the hospital.

" 'Tweren't bad," Terry admitted, "but I got browned off with lying so still like, and nothing to look at but them streets. And here 'tis just as bad—nothing to look at but that there wall; the window be too high up to see out of, and if I could, there'd be nothing to see 'cept the side of the hollow."

"But couldn't we carry your bed outside?" I asked, looking doubtfully at the heavy iron bedstead on which he lay.

He shook his head.

"Couldn't get it through the door without taking it to pieces," he replied gloomily, "and yer can't move me off it—me back hurts too bad."

"Haven't you any books?" we asked.

"I ain't much hand at reading," he answered, "although maybe I'd enjoy 'em if they'd pictures in. What I wants to see is them hills and birds and animals, and things."

His voice shook a little, and his big eyes filled with

tears. Poor, tired, cross little Terry! We both felt dreadfully sorry for him, but we didn't know how to comfort him.

"I'll bring you all my bird books," said Philip, who was looking most upset. "We'll come ever so often and tell you what things are looking like, and then when we've gone you can shut your eyes and pretend you're seeing them. I'll tell you what Tanglewoods look like now, when we came over the hills this afternoon. They haven't got in the second mowings yet, so the hay is still lying out in the fields. The hops will soon be ripe and are beginning to smell when you go past the yards. The apples in the orchard are beginning to turn rosy and weigh down the branches. Oh, and I think they will cut the harvests very soon because the wheat is ripe and the wind makes nice noises in it. I saw Mr. Lake getting out his tractor, and there are lots of flowers—scabious, and poppies, and knapweeds, and bedstraws and things; we'll bring you some next time, and some apples."

Terry seemed pleased; a faint pink tinge crept into his almost colorless cheeks.

"You goin' to the hop fields?" he asked wistfully.

"We might," I answered, "if Auntie will let us—we could earn some money then, couldn't we, Philip?—to help with the camera."

"I used to earn a heap of money down at the hopyards," said Terry. " 'Nuff to buy me a pair of winter boots. Mum'll have to try and go this year, but she can't leave me long, and she's had to give up her work to stop and mind me."

"The gypsies are arriving already," I went on eagerly. "I saw them putting up camp outside a lovely little yellow trailer with lots of little children with black hair. They were tumbling up and down the steps. They're camping in Mr. Lane's field. I'd love to be a gypsy, wouldn't you?"

But Terry, who knew much more than I did about gypsies, shook his head darkly.

"You be thankful fer what yer are," he advised, wisely.

We found no further difficulty in thinking of things to say—indeed we talked so much that we stayed much longer than we meant to, and were interrupted by Terry's mother coming in with his tea.

Terry's meal consisted of a cup of very strong tea and a crust thinly spread with margarine, on a chipped old plate. It did not look at all appetizing to me, but it reminded me of the chocolate I'd brought. It had begun to melt in my pocket, but it was still very nice, and Terry's eyes absolutely gleamed when he saw it. We did not give him the catapult because it did not seem as though it would be any use—his arms looked too thin and white to aim with it.

"Terry," asked Philip just as we were leaving, "when are you going to be able to get up and play with us again?"

He did not answer for a minute, but the frightened, unhappy look came back into his eyes.

"Maybe never," he whispered. "They thinks I don't know, but down at the 'ospital I 'eard the doctor talking to the nurse, and 'e said, 'It's all up with 'im, poor little chap—I can't do nuffing more for 'im.' And I thinks maybe that's why they let my mum take me 'ome. They can't do nuffing more to make me better."

We were horrified to hear this, and once again we could think of nothing to say to comfort him. So we left him rather sadly; but just as we were going out of the door he called after us:

"When 'yer comin' again?"

"We can't come tomorrow," answered Philip, "because we've got to go to the dentist. But we'll come the day after and bring the bird books."

"For certain sure?" called Terry.

"For certain sure," we called back.

Terry's mother was out in the hollow hanging up a torn little nightshirt on the clothesline; she gave us a surly glance but did not speak. When we said "Good afternoon" she only grunted.

"What a cross woman!" I remarked, as we climbed the hollow. "I'm glad she's not my mother."

We were very silent on the way home, because we were both feeling so sorry for Terry and we were both wondering what we could do to make his life happier. Nothing we could think of seemed much good, because nothing could make up for having to lie all day in a dark, stuffy room, staring at the wall, while the apples ripened, and the harvest fields rustled outside.

As I walked home that hazy summer day, I realized for the first time how thankful I ought to be for the things that I had always taken for granted. I had never thought about it before, but now I suddenly became aware of my strong little arms and legs, and my warm healthy body. I paused on the summit of the ridge and looked away to the far Welsh hills. I listened a moment to the crickets chirping all round me and the chugging of a tractor in the ripe corn; then for one glad moment my heart suddenly rose up in gratitude to God because I had eyes to see, and ears to hear, and feet to run.

Chapter 16

A MOONLIGHT EXPEDITION

W E WENT TO SEE Terry often and I believe that it was only our visits that kept him alive through those long dark days when he lay flat on his aching back, staring at the wall. Philip lent him all his most precious nature books, and we took him chocolate, and baskets of fruit from the orchard. We felt well rewarded every time by the faint pink of pleasure on his white cheeks and the happiness that would light up his eyes. He never thanked us in words, and his mother still stared at us as though she hated us. We knew nevertheless that Terry's waking hours were spent wondering if we would come, and that he lay from dinnertime onward with his eyes fastened on the door and his ears straining for the sound of our footsteps.

We had told Aunt Margaret about him, and once or twice she had sent him little presents. Aunt Margaret and I were slowly getting to understand each other, and

I no longer tried to wriggle out of helping her in the mornings. At first I had done my jobs because I thought I ought to, but after a few days I found that housework was really fun, as long as I was doing my best and not trying to get out of it all the time. My aunt said nothing, but I knew she was pleased at the change. Gradually we grew fond of each other and I began to talk to her more freely, instead of keeping everything a secret.

Uncle Peter was interested in Terry, too, and once or twice he had taken the step-ladder to the orchard and picked enormous rosy apples that grew right at the top of the tree against the sky, for us to take to him. They were the size of big grapefruit; when they were polished up we could see our faces in their shiny skins. Terry loved them, and even his mother looked interested.

"Did yer pick those there in your garden?" she asked suddenly one afternoon, as we placed one of them between Terry's small white hands.

We jumped, for except for her first greeting it was the first time she had ever spoken to us. We turned smiling toward her, for we wanted her to come to like us as much as Terry did.

"Yes," I answered, "we've lots of trees full of big, shiny apples like these. We shall be picking them in about a week, and then we'll bring some more; but we picked these early because we thought Terry would like them."

She only grunted and turned away, but I could not help feeling pleased she had spoken to us and admired our apples. I thought I would try and talk to her again.

The nights were very hot, and owing to the extra "Summer Time" it did not get dark until very late. Philip and I used to kick our bedclothes off and lie in our night things by the open windows trying to get cool. Often I got tired of lying alone, and would go and sit on his bed; we would talk until the cool darkness gathered round us and we felt ready for sleep.

It was on one of these hot, still nights, when the sky was still red with the last glow of sunset, that I tiptoed across the hall and found Philip with his head out of the window. I pushed him a little and stuck my head out beside his; a breath of air seemed to move toward us from the hills, bringing with it the cry of a sheep somewhere up among the rocks.

"I don't think I shall be able to go to sleep all night, Phil," I remarked. "It's such a beautiful night I seem to want to look out of the window all the time. It's full moon, too—look, I can see it coming up behind that fir tree."

We watched the moon climb above the horizon, almost blood-red in color; it seemed all tangled up in the black boughs of the fir, but soon it would steer clear and all the world would be flooded with soft silver light. I turned suddenly on Philip, my head full of moonlight.

"Phil!" I whispered excitedly. "Have you ever been out on the hills at night?"

"No," answered Philip, "I haven't—not proper night. Why?"

"Oh, Philip," I breathed, giving his arm a little squeeze, "let's go now, just out through the hedge and up above the quarry. It would be so beautiful—just you and me, and the big yellow moon. Come on, Phil!"

Philip hesitated. "Do you think it would be very naughty?" he asked. "After all, you know, we were going to try to be good."

"I know," I urged. "And we really have been rather good, too—at least I've been cross with Aunt Margaret once or twice, but last holidays I was cross nearly every day. And it isn't really a bit naughty either—after all, what's naughty in wanting to see the moon? It's not hurting anyone and it's not even being disobedient, because Aunt Margaret has never actually told us not to go out at night and look at the moon."

Philip thought this over for a minute or two. It seemed to strike him as sensible, for all he said was, "Are you going to dress properly?"

"Oh, no," I said, "I shan't bother—I shall tuck my nightie up and put on my coat. You put on your Sunday trousers, those long ones, over your pajamas, and put on your coat, too."

This was no sooner said than done, and, looking rather lumpy about the lower quarters, with our handkerchiefs stuffed in our mouths because we wanted to giggle, Philip and I tiptoed down to the front door and turned the key. It creaked and grated alarmingly, but my uncle and aunt must have been very soundly asleep, for although we stood rooted to the spot for several moments nothing happened.

We shut the door noiselessly behind us and stepped out into the open. Then we both stopped and looked round, because the world seemed so strange and different, and the sky with its millions of stars looked so far away. I slipped my hand into Philip's as I always did when things seemed strange, and together we tiptoed through the shadowed orchard towards our gap. The shadows of the apple boughs looked so fierce and frightening that I almost ran back—only Philip, having made up his mind, kept going.

Out through the gap and up the stony track that led to the hills we went without a word—up the steps behind the clock tower, over the first group of grey rocks—and we were there, standing on the lower slopes by moonlight, with the silver world lying at our feet.

"Come on!" whispered Philip, and seizing my hand again he began to climb.

We climbed in silence until we reached the very top of the North Hill and stood by the little heap of stones that marked the summit. The wind came sweeping up the valleys, clean and pure, and laden with the scents of evergreen shrubs and fern; a sheep lifted its head at the sound of our footsteps and bleated a warning to the stars—otherwise all was silent. We sat down on the heap to look.

There was such a tremendous lot to see in spite of the darkness. Behind, there were the black shapes of the beacon and the camp rising up into the night, and dark ranges of wooded hills massed beyond them. In front of us stretched the plains dotted with points of light, and every river and pond gleamed in the moonlight like some silver fairy lake.

But mostly we looked up because we both loved stars, and tonight they all shone clearly, right over the vast panorama of the sky. There was the Milky Way rambling from east to west like a misty banner. High up in the north the Pole Star looked down on mariners at sea. Right above us clustered the Pleiades, and Cassiopeia shaped like an M. We pointed them out to each

other with eager fingers and felt how wonderful it was
to be up there, alone with the stars.

We stayed a long time, until Philip remarked that he
thought we'd better go back, as it would soon be morning and we should be so tired next day. Actually it was
not quite as bad as that, for when we reached the
bottom of the hill, the clock on the tower struck one—
and nearly made us jump.

We sang all the way down because we knew there
was no one to hear us, and it was a relief to make a
noise after that stillness. We sang all the songs we
could remember, mostly about seas and ships and one
about a mermaid who lured mariners to their death.
While we sang we jumped over bushes, or leaped from
one rock to the other like two mountain goats.

But when we got back to the stony track we suddenly
felt tired and thought how nice it would be to cuddle
down into bed and go to sleep. A heaviness seemed to
be stealing over my eyes and I longed for my pillow—only another five minutes and I should lay down
my head and forget everything till morning. I gave a
great big yawn and Philip did the same.

"Now," said Philip, "in through the gap and very,
very quietly across the orchard. How awful if auntie has
noticed! We must absolutely creep."

We were right through the gap, and well into the

orchard when Philip suddenly stopped dead and dug his finger-nails into my arm. With the other hand he pointed, and as I followed his finger my heart seemed to turn right over. I only just stopped myself from screaming.

Chapter 17

A MIDNIGHT ADVENTURE

A TALL FIGURE in a dark cloak was moving toward us through the trees, bowed under the weight of a sack.

She had not seen us, for we had come very quietly, and we stood hidden in the deep shadows of the apple trees. The figure was making for the gap, and in a few minutes must pass right by where we stood. I think I should have fainted outright if it had not been for Philip, who seemed much less frightened than I was.

"It's a woman stealing apples," he breathed. "We ought to try and stop her. They're auntie's apples and she's got a great big sackful."

I could not argue or tell him to stop, because I was much too scared to speak. But I clung tightly to Philip and was sort of dragged with him when he suddenly stepped out into the open to confront the figure, who was nearly upon us. The moonlight shone full on her

173

face, and we recognized her in a flash. It was Terry's mother!

She gave a short, terrified shriek and dropped the sack, so that the apples rolled out and scattered in all directions. Then she cowered down in the grass, and covered her face with her cloak and began mumbling words very fast, almost as though she were saying her prayers. Neither Philip nor I knew what to do, until she suddenly flung back her fierce, proud head and spoke to us.

"So ye'd be a-spying on me by night even, would ye?" she hissed, shaking her fist at us. "And now ye'll be sending the police after me tomorrer and they'll take me from my poor dyin' boy. You, with yer fine food, and yer grand clothing, yer can't spare the price of a few apples for my laddie what's starvin' and cold—and him a-dyin' before my very eyes, and me with nothing ter give him—oh! Terry, Terry, they'll take me from you . . ." She hid her face in her cloak again and burst into bitter, passionate weeping.

I looked at Philip, feeling more troubled than I had ever felt before. Philip was frowning, too, as though he was wondering what to do next. Presently, however, he made up his mind, for he suddenly squatted down in the grass beside the poor huddled figure, and tried to draw her hands from her face.

"We weren't spying on you," he said, gently, "we were only here by accident, 'cos we wanted to see the moon. Of course you ought not to be taking auntie's apples, but if Terry is really cold and starving we certainly won't tell. We should hate you to be put in prison and there be no one to look after him."

The woman had stopped sobbing, and was looking intently at him, with a gleam of hope in her wild eyes.

"Little gentleman," she answered in a trembling voice, taking hold of him in her eagerness, "listen to me! I swear before God I'll never come again. I know I'm a wicked woman and I didn't oughter have come, but my Terry's a-dyin' and the doctor he says to me, you get 'im extra milk and a warm blanket for the winter, and you feed 'im up proper if you wants to keep him a little longer. And my Terry, he's all that I've got. His dad left me, and his little sister's in 'er grave; and now as 'e's 'elpless I can't leave him to work for 'im days, and 'ow can I get 'im wot 'e needs? They'll take 'im from me and put 'im back in the 'ospital. Oh! Little lady and gentleman, don't tell on me this once—don't have my Terry took from me, or me took from my Terry!"

She was kneeling in the grass, clasping her hands almost as though she were praying to us.

I wanted to say that of course we wouldn't tell, and

she could have all the apples she wanted, because I felt so sorry for her, but Philip stopped me.

"We won't tell," he said slowly, "but if you really stop stealing, as you say, I can't see how you are going to get any money. And yet, of course, it is awfully wicked to steal. Won't anybody give you any money?"

She shook her head.

"If I applied for relief they'd only put Terry back in the 'ospital where I couldn't get at 'im. They'd say our house weren't fit for a sick child, and no more 'tis—but we're together. That's wot we wants."

She looked at us hungrily, as though pleading with us to understand. Philip still seemed wrapped in thought.

"Listen!" he said at last, in his most earnest voice, "I think I've got a sort of an idea; but I can't tell you about it now. You go back to Terry, and we'll come and see you tomorrow when we've talked about it—but we've promised not to tell, haven't we, Ruth?"

"Oh, yes," I agreed, "we won't say anything and we'll come tomorrow."

"God bless you, little lady and gentleman," whispered Terry's mother, "and forgive me for being a wicked woman."

She picked up her empty sack and was gone through

the gap in the hedge before we had time to say good night. We were left gazing down at the scattered fruit.

"I wish we'd let her have them," I remarked.

"No," said Philip. "It's Uncle Peter's fruit and it would have been as bad as stealing ourselves if we'd given it to her. I've thought of something else, Ruth, but I'll tell you in the morning. I'm so tired, and I want to go back to bed."

I was very tired, too, so I asked him no further questions. We crept upstairs and tumbled into bed; I was just falling asleep when Philip's head came around the door.

"How much is there in the money-box?" he whispered.

"About nine dollars," I murmured back drowsily, and the next moment I was deep in the land of dreams.

Chapter 18

ABOUT GIVING

O F COURSE WE BOTH overslept next morning and were awakened only by the ringing of the breakfast gong and the sound of my aunt's footsteps coming up to see what had happened. She was rather suspicious at the sight of us just waking up.

"It's my belief you don't settle properly at night," she remarked severely, "or you'd be awake at the proper time. I believe there's a lot of running about when you should be tucked up, and I won't have it. Once in bed, you're to stay in bed, or I shall have to start locking you in."

Philip and I looked at each other guiltily out of the corners of our eyes. We hoped our aunt would not say any more on the subject; fortunately it was washing day, and she was very busy, so no more questions were asked.

I was simply longing for a good talk with Philip, but

felt that I had really been so naughty the night before, in spite of all my excuses, that I had better try to be extra good today to make up. So I presented myself in the kitchen and offered to turn the mangle, and my aunt was pleased. We chatted together in a friendly way while we worked, and I couldn't help thinking how nice it was to have Aunt Margaret talking to me almost as though I was grown up; she never used to do it, and I began to wonder how it was that things were different.

"I think it has all to do with the Good Shepherd," I thought to myself as I hung out the handkerchiefs. "It really has been different since Philip and I began to know about Him. I do believe He really is beginning to make me less cross and less lazy, and I do believe Aunt Margaret is getting nicer, too. Perhaps after we've been to see Terry this afternoon we might tell Aunt Margaret more about him, and ask her if she has a blanket to spare so he wouldn't be cold in the winter."

Thinking of Terry made me think of his mother again—as, indeed, I'd been thinking of her most of the morning. Her last sad words came back into my mind and said themselves over and over again:

"God forgive me for being a wicked woman!"

Of course God would forgive her if she really asked, because if she was a wicked woman who stole things,

she was just like that poor sheep on the precipice, and
therefore the Good Shepherd was certainly looking for
her. I wondered if she knew about that, because if not,
perhaps I had better try to tell her. If she belonged to
the Good Shepherd it would probably make a lot of
difference to her. He would look after her and Terry,
and she could ask Him for blankets and extra milk.

I was thinking so hard about this that I had quite
forgotten the handkerchiefs until Aunt Margaret put
her head out of the window to see what was happening.

"Come along, Ruth!" she called. "Think what you're
doing; you've been standing there doing nothing the
last three or four minutes."

I turned very pink and went on with my work in a
great hurry. But I was longing to finish and get to
Philip and tell him about my plan, and, fortunately for
me, the wash was nearly over.

"You can go now," said Aunt Margaret, taking off
her apron. "You've been a great help this morning, so
you must have a good game before dinner."

I scuttled upstairs two steps at a time, and found
Philip lying flat on his bed with all the contents of his
money-box spread out in front of him. I knelt down
and we counted it together.

"Almost nine dollars," observed Philip thoughtfully,
"and I saw a camera for something over ten dollars. If

we both saved our pocket-money for the rest of the holidays, we could get it by the beginning of term."

There was a pause, and I watched him anxiously.

"On the other hand," went on Philip, "if we gave Terry two dollars for extra milk, we could get it round about Christmas."

He gave a little sigh, and I knew he was thinking of the squirrels' dreys and the dormouse nests that we should find when autumn came, and the nests of harvest mice that turned up when the corn was cut. I felt I could not bear it for his sake.

"Oh, but I don't think we need give that much," I cried. "One dollar and a half would buy an awful lot of extra milk, and I vote we ask auntie for a quilt. She's sure to have an old one."

Philip fingered his coins.

"Well," he said, "I really don't think we need decide now. We can think it out on the way. I'll take the whole money-box, and then if I want to give her more or less, I can!"

I agreed that it was too important a matter to decide in a hurry, and we put the money back. I wanted to tell about my plan.

"Philip," I began, "do you remember Terry's mother saying she was a wicked woman?"

"Well, she is rather," agreed Philip. "I mean, I'm

very sorry for her, but however poor you are it's still very wicked to steal other people's apples."

"Yes, I know," I went on, "but I was just thinking, Philip, if she's really wicked don't you think we ought to try to tell her about the Good Shepherd? She might not know that He's looking for her, and could forgive her and make her good—and I think she'd be much happier if she knew, as I was."

Philip nodded.

"I thought of that myself," he admitted, "and I really think we ought to try—but she may not want to listen; grown-ups don't always. I saw a poor old tramp sitting by the road on my way home from school last term, and he looked so very miserable that I thought I would go and tell him that Jesus loved him; but he told me to mind my own business, and it was boots and beer he wanted, no Bibles."

"What did you say then?" I asked, deeply interested.

"Well, I couldn't say much," answered Philip. "I just told him I hadn't any beer and my boots wouldn't fit him, and he told me to stop being saucy and run along. He just didn't want to hear about Jesus, so I had to go away."

"Well," I answered, "I suppose Mrs. Terry may be like that, but I think we'd better try, all the same. She may not be."

We set off after dinner along the well-trodden way that led to Terry's house. I carried a Bible and my picture tucked inside; Philip carried the money-box, which was most satisfyingly heavy and jingled as we walked; but he was rather depressed, and I thought he must be hankering after the camera, so I longed to comfort him.

"Philip," I said, "I think one dollar might buy quite a lot of extra milk. Let's ask how much extra milk costs."

Philip only grunted; he didn't seem to want to talk about it at all, so we walked on in silence.

We were halfway down the hill toward the hollow when Terry's mother suddenly appeared from behind a tree, where she seemed to have been waiting for us. She looked at us very anxiously, as though we might have forgotten our promise.

"Thought we might have our bit of a talk out here," she began nervously, "before you goes on down to Terry. You won't be telling my Terry nothing about them apples, will you now? I did it for his sake, but he'd take on something terrible if he knowed; he's a good straight lad, is Terry."

"Of course we won't tell Terry," Philip assured her. "We promised we wouldn't tell anyone. Let's talk here on the hill, and then he won't be able to hear us."

We sat down among the harebells, and were silent for a little while. Philip looked at me because he was expecting me to begin. I looked at the ground because I was shy, and Terry's mother looked very hard at the money-box.

Philip kicked me and nodded, because he really thought it was time somebody said something. So I drew out my picture from between the pages of my Bible and held it in front of her. It was worn and frayed at the edges because I had looked at it so often, but to me it was beautiful.

"Mrs. Terry," I said shyly, quite forgetting that that was not her name at all, "it can be all right about your stealing those apples if you like, because that Good Shepherd in the picture is Jesus, who died so that we could be forgiven; and that poor sheep on the precipice is us when we do wrong things and run away from God. So if you asked Him, He would forgive you at once and then you could belong to Him, like me and Philip do, and then I think He would help you look after Terry and find money and food for him."

She had been looking more at the money-box than at the picture, but now she turned and stared at me with the greatest curiosity.

"You're a little 'un to be talking good like that, ain't you?" she remarked.

"Oh, no!" I cried, blushing again. "It's not me who says it—I didn't make it up—it's all in the Bible. Look, I'll read you the story. It sounds much better in the Bible than when I tell it."

I found the fifteenth chapter of Luke and read the story slowly and reverently. " 'There is joy in the presence of the angels of God over one sinner that repenteth'—that's like I told you, Mrs. Terry—God and all the angels are happy when we ask the Shepherd to find us."

Terry's mother was listening by now. "It's like what they learned us in Sunday School when I was a little kid your age," she mumbled.

"Is it?" I answered, much pleased. "Then I'll read you some more"—and I turned to the tenth of John and started on the well-loved chapter that I nearly knew by heart:

" 'I am the Good Shepherd; the Good Shepherd giveth his life for the sheep.' "

I stopped short because a dreadful new idea had suddenly come into my head.

The Good Shepherd had given His life—every single thing that He possessed—for the sheep, and I didn't really want to give even a dollar.

If only I could make Philip understand that it must be two dollars! I coughed and made faces at him, but he wouldn't look at me. He was slowly unfastening the money-box. Terry's mother was watching.

I gave him a little kick, but he still wouldn't look at me. What if he took me at my word and gave only one dollar, when the Good Shepherd had given His life? If only I could make him understand!

Philip moved nearer to Terry's mother.

"We've brought you some money to buy milk and bedclothes for Terry," he said simply. "It's not very much, but it's all we've got," and so saying, he tipped up the money-box and emptied the money into Terry's mother's apron.

"It's about nine dollars," he said distinctly, so that there might be no mistake about it, "and we hope it will do Terry a lot of good. Now we will go down to the cottage and see him for a little bit."

He stood up and started off down the hill, but I stayed behind for a moment. The Good Shepherd had given His life; Philip had given all the money for his camera—I wanted to give something, too. I suddenly remembered that my most precious possession was in my hands. So I opened the Bible and pulled it out, and laid it with the coins on the black apron.

"It's my picture," I said softly. "And you can have it to remind you about the Good Shepherd wanting to find you."

"Thank you, little lady," she replied, and I left her sitting there counting her coins on the hillside, while I ran after Philip.

"I hope you don't mind that I gave all the money," said Philip, as we were walking home an hour later. "After all, a lot of it was yours really, but somehow I felt we couldn't keep it—I mean the camera doesn't seem to matter much compared with Terry, when you come to think of it, does it?"

"No," I agreed, "and the funny part is, I was thinking the same thing. When we came to the bit about the Good Shepherd giving His life, it seemed awful to be giving such a little, and I was trying to make you look at me—to tell you to give more."

"Funny," said Philip, "I thought I should feel miserable without my money, but actually I feel awfully happy."

"Funny!" I agreed. "I thought it would be terrible giving away my picture, but I sort of feel glad she's got it now. Isn't it queer?"

"Yes," said Philip. "We never guessed it would be so nice, but when you come to think of it, Ruth, I believe it's the first time we've given away anything that we really wanted to keep badly, so we couldn't have known."

We walked on in silence thinking about it.

Chapter 19

HOPS AND MUSHROOMS

THE SUMMER HOLIDAYS were specially exciting that year, because my aunt gave us permission for the first time to spend certain afternoons in the hop fields, where we earned quite a lot of money. We had given up saving for the camera for the present, and our idea was to earn the price of a warm blanket for Terry. We had told Aunt Margaret about it, and this was her suggestion, as she hadn't actually got one to spare. But she gave us other little things for him, and mended up Philip's old pajamas, which were flannel and warm and would be much more comfortable than his thin little cotton nightshirts.

Mr. Robinson had also promised to go and see Terry. On one of our many Saturday visits, Philip and I had told him about Terry and had begged him to call.

"You see," I explained, "I've tried to tell him about the Good Shepherd, but he doesn't want to listen. He

says if God loved him He'd make his back better and
let him run about again, and when he said that, I didn't
know what to say—but if you came, you could explain
it all, I expect, couldn't you?"

Mr. Robinson had smiled.

"No," he answered, "I couldn't explain it at all,
because when God sends sad things into our lives He
often doesn't tell us why. He just tells us that it is the
best thing for us. If we really love Him we believe
what He says even if we don't understand. That is what
'trusting' means. In any case, Terry would probably
listen to you more than he would to me, because you
are a child like himself and I'm only a grown-up."

"But he doesn't listen," I had insisted. "He doesn't
take any notice of me at all; he just tells me to talk
about something else."

"Well, then," Mr. Robinson had replied, "you must
start praying every day that he will listen. God doesn't
always answer our prayers at once, but He hears them,
and if they are right prayers He always answers them in
the end—and I will come and visit the little boy when
I come home again, and see what I can do for him."

So Mr. and Mrs. Robinson and the twins had gone
off on their holiday and would not be back for three
weeks. In the meantime Philip and I earned what we
could in the hop fields. We loved the hop fields with

the noisy pickers and the strange smell that clung to our clothes and fingers. We sat around a bale with a family to whom we had attached ourselves, and listened to their friendly chatter while we picked. At six o'clock we would line up for our pay and feel wonderfully important and grown-up when our money was handed to us.

Once this family invited us to stay to supper with them, and we sat around a brazier of glowing coals. They cooked a queer sort of pancake in a big frying pan. It smelled delicious, and when it was tossed on a tin plate and handed to us we thought we had never tasted anything so good. But Aunt Margaret was cross with us because we got home so late, and when we explained she was crosser still, and said goodness knows what we might catch if we went sitting around and eating off tin plates with gypsies. So that delight had to be given up.

We found another way of earning money, too, which Aunt Margaret thought a better way than hop-picking—she was always a little nervous of our catching things or hearing bad language in the hop-yards. But one misty September morning we got up early and ran out into the silver fields where the spiders were festooning the grasses with their webs. We took off our shoes and stockings because we liked the feel of cold dew between our toes, and were skipping up and down the field, when Philip suddenly stopped; he had caught sight of a little white button mushroom and stooped down to look underneath and make sure it wasn't a puff ball.

"Mushrooms, Ruth!" he called. "Let's see if we can find some more!"

We found lots more—in fact, the field was full of them—tight buttons and big umbrellas—and we heaped them up until we could have filled a whole basket full, only we had no basket.

"There's only one thing to be done," Philip remarked. "You must take off your blouse and tie the sleeves in a knot so that it makes a bag. We must get these mushrooms home somehow."

So I retired behind a willow tree in case any neighboring farmers might appear, or in case, as Philip said, I might shock the cows; and when my blouse had been filled up with mushrooms it began to stretch, and by the time we reached home it had grown so long that it almost touched the ground. We were going to give some to Aunt Margaret to cook and we were going to ask whether we might sell the rest to the greengrocer up the road.

Aunt Margaret was pleased with the mushrooms, but she was not at all pleased with my blouse. She said it was enough to give me a bad chill. So I was given a dose of cold mixture and made to wash the blouse, and was rather sulky all breakfast in consequence.

But I cheered up later, because when we asked Aunt Margaret if we might sell the rest of our mushrooms to Mr. Daniels the greengrocer, she said she did not mind at all, provided we took them in a proper basket. So we set out excited, presented ourselves at the counter, and asked to see Mr. Daniels personally.

Mr. Daniels was fat and bald, and wore horn-rimmed spectacles on the end of a large red nose. He liked Philip and me, and beamed at us over the counter. When he saw our mushrooms he threw up his hands in admiration.

"Dearie me!" said Mr. Daniels. "There's a clever little lady and gentleman! Now I'll weigh 'em out and pay you same as I pay the farmers, and if you find any more you bring 'em along to Mr. Daniels!"

We did find lots more, and what with mushrooms and hops, the money-box began to get really heavy again, and we were beginning to talk about the color of the blanket we would buy, when a wonderful thing happened.

We had wandered over the hills in the heat to take Terry some Victoria plums, and we found him alone; the cabin was particularly stuffy, and Terry looked hot and flushed; his dark hair lay damp on his forehead, and he had thrown all his bedclothes back. He did not notice us come in because he was staring so hard at the wall opposite, where his mother had hung the picture I had given her.

"Hullo, Terry!" we greeted him, sitting down on the bed. "Is your mother out?"

"Mm," answered Terry, wearily. Poor Terry! He seemed so exhausted that even our arrival had failed to cheer him up. "Her's been gone a long time."

"Where to?" we asked.

"Dunno," replied Terry. "Her wouldn't say."

There was a pause, then Terry spoke again in a fretful voice.

"Take that there picture away with you!" he commanded. "It bothers my mum awful. Last few days she's kinder cried when she's looked at it; she was happier before you brought it, and we don't want it."

"But I can't take it away," I objected. "It's your mother's—I gave it to her; it would be sort of stealing to take it away."

Terry passed his hand wearily over his forehead and turned his face to the wall.

"Wish I was dead," he muttered.

We had never seen Terry quite so discouraged before, and we longed to comfort him; but what could we say to comfort a boy who had to lie in this hot, cheerless gloom all day long? Even when we offered him a plum he pushed it away.

"I'm feelin' sick," he explained. "Maybe I'll eat it later."

We left very soon, because he seemed too tired to want us. His mother had not returned, and we felt very depressed as we climbed the hill.

"Philip," I said, "do you still pray every day that Terry will get better?"

"Not *every* day," answered Philip, "because sometimes I feel sure he won't—I mean perhaps God thinks he'd better not get better. The doctor said he wouldn't, you know, and doctors are usually right."

"But God could do a miracle," I insisted, "like He did in the Bible—it seems too awful, doesn't it? Terry seems sadder every time we go."

"It isn't really being ill that's the worst part," Philip observed thoughtfully; "it's that awful little house. It's so hot and dark, and there's a sort of not very nice smell about it and it must be dull. If he could be ill somewhere nice it would be different."

But I could see no way out of this difficulty at all, unless we prayed that someone with a nice house would adopt Terry—and, on further thought, we decided not

to pray for that after all, as Terry would hate to leave
his mother and his mother would hate to lose him.

We were talking so earnestly about it all when we
reached the gate that we did not look where we were
going and nearly bumped into my aunt, who was coming down the path talking to a tall woman in a dark
cloak. We looked up quickly into the visitor's face, and
to our utter astonishment we saw that the tall woman
was Terry's mother, and her dark eyes were red with
weeping. And, stranger still, my aunt, who was gener-
ally extremely severe with beggars and gypsies, was
talking gently to her and had laid her hand on her arm.

They neither of them took any notice of us, and we
went indoors quickly because we somehow felt that
Terry's mother hadn't really wanted to meet us at all.
Once inside we looked at each other in astonishment.
What could my aunt and Terry's mother have been
saying to each other? "Perhaps she's asking for things
for Terry," I suggested.

Philip shook his head.

"I don't think it's that," he said, "because Auntie was
being so nice to her, and usually she's rather cross with
beggars."

If we had hopes that my aunt would explain things,
we were disappointed. She came back into the house a
few minutes later and went upstairs to her bedroom.

When she came down she was very quiet and took no notice of us at all. I thought her face was sadder than usual, and although she started cooking the supper she looked as though she was thinking of something that wasn't supper at all!

Next day at breakfast another surprise awaited us. My aunt laid down her knife and fork and looked at her watch.

"Ruth," she announced, "I am going out for the morning; it is very important and I shall probably not be back for hours, so I am going to let you get the dinner. The potatoes are peeled, and there is cold meat, so you will only have to wash the lettuce, and peel and stew the apples and make some custard. I showed you how to make custard the other day, so it will be a good chance for you to try."

Philip and I stared at her in astonishment. Never before, that we could remember, had our aunt gone out for the morning, or missed cooking the dinner. It must have been dreadfully important business that called her, and we were extremely curious to know what it could be. However, of course, we didn't ask, and I felt so proud at being allowed to cook the dinner all by myself that I soon forgot to wonder.

Aunt Margaret was as good as her word. She got up from the breakfast table, put on her hat, and walked

straight out of the front door—and that was the last
that we saw of her until dinnertime.

Philip and I, left to ourselves, went to work with a
will. Being mistress of the house for the morning rather
appealed to me. We carried the breakfast things out
and started to wash up feeling tremendously important.
I began by tipping nearly a whole jar of soap flakes into
the bowl and whisking until the foam stood up nearly
as high as the faucets—and after that, of course, we had
to spend ten minutes or so scooping it up with our
hands and blowing soap bubbles all over the kitchen,
squealing with delight as they landed on the top
shelves. Then I suddenly remembered that I was not behaving, so I turned to the sink in a great hurry and
plunged my elbows into the soapy flakes and began
fishing for the silver.

The morning passed very pleasantly. Philip and I
peeled enough apples to feed a regiment. Although I
burned our saucepan badly while making the custard, it
didn't taste too burned. We caught three little slugs in
the lettuce and carried them carefully back to the lettuce patch in case their mothers should be missing
them; then when dinner was ready to our satisfaction
we started on the housework. We took all the rugs into
the garden and danced up and down with them, smoth-
ering ourselves with dust. Yes, it was certainly great

fun being left in charge of the house. The morning went quickly and it seemed only a very short time before my aunt walked in at the gate. It was dinner-time.

I made a dive for the potatoes, which were boiling merrily, and the dinner was served up by a very flushed, untidy little cook, who had to be sent away from the table to brush her hair the minute grace had been said.

However, my aunt seemed pleased with my efforts; she praised the potatoes and salad and said nothing about the burned flavor of the custard. She looked happy, too; much happier than she had looked at breakfast, and now and then we noticed her smiling to herself as though she had some very nice secret.

"I hope you enjoyed yourself this morning, Auntie," said Philip politely.

Aunt Margaret's eyes twinkled, and the little smile played round the corners of her mouth again.

"I've enjoyed myself very much indeed, thank you, Philip," she replied solemnly; then after a moment she added:

"Tonight when Uncle Peter comes home, and I've talked to him, I'm going to tell you about it; but till then it's a secret."

Philip and I were very interested. When evening

came we kept running out into the road to see if Uncle
were coming. When at last we saw him approaching
we tore madly into the kitchen.

"He's coming, Auntie," we shouted; "now, the
secret, the secret!"

She shooed us both out of the kitchen with a wooden
spoon.

"Get along with you," she said. "I can't make fish
cakes and talk secrets at the same time. You tell your
uncle to come here, and then you run out in the garden."

So Uncle Peter went in and shut the door.

Chapter 20

THE SECRET

Now FOR THE SECRET!" we exclaimed, and settled ourselves comfortably on the stools at my aunt's feet.

We were sitting in the summer twilight just outside the French windows, and the air was sweet with the scent of late roses, while bats fluttered by on restless wings. My aunt leaned forward in her chair while she talked, and as the story went on, we crept closer and closer until our heads were resting against her knees.

"Well," she said, "before we start talking about secrets, I want to know what you were doing in the orchard at one o'clock in the morning a few weeks ago?"

We both jumped and went very red; this was most unexpected. But strange to say Auntie did not sound particularly cross; in fact, there was a tiny shake in her voice that might have meant that she was trying not to laugh.

After a very uncomfortable silence, Philip answered in rather a small voice.

"We couldn't go to sleep that night," he explained, "and we wanted to see the stars close up. So we put some clothes on and went up to the top of the Hill and then . . ."

"You went up to the top of the North Hill, alone in the dark?" interrupted my aunt, aghast.

"You've never actually told us not to," I chimed in quickly.

"Ruth," said my aunt solemnly, "there are a great many things I have never actually told you not to do, but which you know in your heart I shouldn't like, so don't make silly excuses. Now before we go any further I want you to promise me that you will never go out alone again at night as long as you live with me."

We both promised most earnestly.

"Very well then," continued my aunt. "As long as you understand that, we will say no more about it. Now perhaps you are wondering how I came to know about it."

As a matter of fact, we thought we could guess, but we did not say so.

"Yesterday," said my aunt, "just after you had gone

out, Terry's mother came to see me. She had a long
story to tell me. She told me that some weeks ago she
was in despair about earning some extra money to buy a
blanket for her little boy, and when she saw those big
rosy apples you took to Terry she decided to come at
night and help herself. She did this once or twice,
taking a few pounds from each tree so that your uncle
wouldn't notice, and earned quite a little sum by selling
them to the greengrocers in the villages around Tanglewoods. Then one night she met you in the orchard."

We looked guiltily at each other and wondered
whether my aunt would be very cross with us for not
telling. We weren't enjoying this secret much!

"You promised not to tell," went on my aunt,
"which wasn't very sensible of you, because if you had
told me all about it sooner I might have been able to
help her sooner, but still, I know you meant it kindly.
And then she tells me that you went to see her and took
her all your money. And you, Ruth, gave her your
picture."

I blushed again; I was rather bashful about my picture.

"She tells me you sat down beside her and read her
the story of the lost sheep in the Bible, and told her
about the Shepherd who wanted to forgive her and save
her. You seem to have explained your picture rather

well, Ruth, for she took it home and hung it on the
wall. Ever since then she has wanted to be like the
sheep in the picture. But she felt she could not ask God
to forgive her until she had brought me the money
from the apples she had stolen. And so yesterday she
came."

There was a long silence. The moon was rising behind the black pines, and the garden was full of whispering breezes and rustles. We sat quite still with upturned faces waiting for Aunt Margaret to go on.

"She came to see me and brought me the money
because she said she felt as though the Shepherd was
calling her, and she could get no rest until she answered Him. And then we had a long talk and she told
me all about the little boy of hers, who seems to be
dying in that dark hovel of a home; I went to see him
this morning and it's all true. She can't leave him to go
to work, and she won't be parted from him to let him
go back to the hospital, and they are as near starving as
one can be nowadays."

My aunt stared out into the twilight. She seemed to
have almost forgotten us.

"And when she had gone last night, Philip and
Ruth, I think the Shepherd spoke to me, too. I have not
thought about Him much for a long time, but last night
He showed me a lot of things."

My eyes were fixed on my aunt's face, and I had drawn so close that she put her arm around me.

"He showed me a great many things I can't tell you about now, but I will tell you about two of them. He showed me a lot of money lying doing nothing in the bank, and He showed me an empty room all covered up with dust sheets, but with a beautiful window looking out over the plain with the sun shining in through it every morning, and the beech tree just outside."

I gave a little jump. "The best spare bedroom," I whispered.

My aunt nodded. "Yes," she agreed. "The best spare bedroom that's been empty for such a long time. But it's not going to be empty any longer, because we want to use it for the Good Shepherd. So the day after tomorrow Terry and his mother are coming to live here with us for a time. Terry's mother is going to help me in the house, and Terry is going to lie by the window in the spare room and get some color into his cheeks. It will be his very own room, and you and Philip shall help arrange it, and get it ready tomorrow. Would you like that?"

Would we like it? We were both so glad that we could not speak one word, but I think we must have looked our joy, for Aunt Margaret laughed a little and seemed to understand. Philip's eyes at any rate were quite starry with happiness.

So we sat and talked until the moon swung clear of the pines and the last glimmer of light had faded in the west. Uncle Peter came and stood in the doorway and we flung ourselves upon him.

"Do you know?" we shouted joyfully. "Do you know?"

"Of course he knows," said my aunt, laughing. "You don't think I'd turn the house into a hospital without asking him."

So we were hustled off to bed, and were told we needn't even wash, except for faces and hands, because it was so late—which was certainly a perfect end to a perfect day!

We spent most of next day getting the room ready for Terry; we spring-cleaned it ourselves and made up the beds—one in the corner for Terry's mother and one by the window for Terry. We collected our nicest books and toys and arranged them where he could see them, and then hung up our brightest pictures on the walls. We picked the rosiest apples and the yellowest pears and put them in a dish by his bed; then we stood and looked around, and decided that it was quite perfect.

I awoke very early on the morning of the great day, and my first thought was that Terry's room was ready and waiting for him. As I lay there I suddenly thought how nice it would be to go and see it now, all by myself at sunrise, so that I should always be able to imagine what Terry saw when he first awoke.

I slipped out of bed and down the stairs and crept into the spare room, which smelled so clean of soap and polish. It was filled with light, and running to the bed, I wrapped the eiderdown around me, and kneeled with my elbows on the sill and looked out.

Just outside, the beech leaves looked almost transparent because of the golden light shining through them, and the sky behind might have been on fire—it was such a blaze of color. Pink fleecy clouds sailed like coral islands in a golden sea, and the plain was hidden in a silver mist. I had never before seen such a glory of sunrise. When I thought of Terry waking to look at that instead of the dark wall of his hut, it just seemed too much, and I laid my face on my arms and cried. "How funny!" I thought, as the tears ran down my cheeks and trickled through my fingers. "It is all so very beautiful that it is hurting me. When I get too happy it almost begins to feel like sadness."

But after that I smoothed out the eiderdown and went back to my bed, because I had left my handkerchief under my pillow and was in urgent need of it. No sooner had my head touched the pillow than I fell fast asleep, only to awaken an hour later in tremendous spirits; the beautiful sad sunrise seemed like a dream that had passed with the night.

Chapter 21

TERRY ARRIVES

TERRY ARRIVED in an ambulance, at tea-time, and his mother came with him, carrying their few little belongings in an old tin box. My aunt had arranged for the ambulance, and Terry had been lifted and carried as gently as possible, but even so he was tired out. When they laid him in his bed by the open window and his dark eyes turned wistfully to the beech tree, his small face looked as white as the pillow.

My aunt took his mother downstairs. Philip went to help with the tin box, so Terry and I were left alone. His face was turned to the window, and I heard a sound rather like a sob, and I knew that he was crying.

"That's queer," I remarked. "I came in here the other morning and saw the sun coming up, and I cried, too. It's a beautiful window, isn't it, Terry? Do you like it?"

But poor, tired, little Terry was too overcome to

speak; he just lay and looked at the beech with the tears
rolling down his cheeks. At last he controlled himself
and whispered with trembling lips, "It's smashin'!"

His mother came in at that moment with a cup of
hot soup, and knelt down by the bed to feed him; I
thought how much nicer she looked when she was
doing things for Terry than when she wasn't. Her face
seemed to become gentle.

The rest of the summer holidays passed quietly. Terry seemed perfectly happy, and would lie for hours
looking out of his window with his arms thrown around
his head. Everything he saw gave him pleasure, and it
was surprising how much there was to see when you
really began to look for it. There was the beech tree
that grew more vivid every day, and the shapes of the
clouds changing over the plain. He watched the dahlias
opening in the garden below, and the petals falling
from the last roses. During the day troops of eager
swallows flying southward would skim past the sill, and
in the evening moths and bats would hover and flutter
noiselessly in and out. He grew to love every sound and
every shadow. I, with my restless feet and boundless
energy, marveled at his deep content.

Philip was supposed to be working for a scholarship,
so most of his evenings were spent at the diningroom
table with his books spread out in front of him. At

these times I would slip upstairs and sit with Terry. Sometimes I would put the light on and read to him, but sometimes I would perch on the bed, and leaning my elbows on the sill, I would stare out into the twilight and talk.

We talked about a great many things, for Terry, now that he was too ill to do much else, thought a good deal. We often went back to those happy days in the wigwam, and talked about nests and animals. Sometimes we talked about the accident and about the hospital and the dreary days in the dark hut; sometimes about my mother and father, and how pleased they would be to see Terry when they came home. Sometimes we just compared thoughts—the queer thoughts that grown-ups forget about, and that children only tell each other.

"Ruth," said Terry suddenly, as we sat in the twilight one evening, "what's dying like?"

I shuffled my feet uneasily. "Oh, I don't know," I answered, "but I think it's very nice. At least, I think it's just like going to a beautiful place where Jesus is, and where everyone is happy. Why, Terry?"

" 'Cos I 'eard the doctor in the 'ospital say it," said Terry, looking round to see that no one else was going to come in at the door. "I told you once. He said, 'It's all up with 'im, poor little chap!'—and that means dyin'."

"But that was a long time ago," I objected.

He shrugged his thin shoulders.

"I ain't no better," he replied. "Ruth, do everybody go there?"

"I'm not sure," I answered slowly. "I think perhaps you have to ask the Shepherd to find you. I think you have to belong to Him. But that is quite easy, Terry. You only have to ask to be found, like the sheep in the picture."

He frowned.

"I were a bad boy," he admitted, doubtfully. "I pinched ever such a lot of things whenever I could lay hands on 'em. The cops nearly got me once."

"I think it would be all right, all the same," I assured him. "But, Terry, I'll ask Mr. Robinson to come and see you. He could tell you about it ever so much better than me."

There was a pause; Terry didn't seem particularly cheered by the prospect of Mr. Robinson.

"Ruth," he said at last, "where's the picture—the one you gived us?"

"Oh, you mean my picture," I answered. "I don't know, Terry; I suppose your mother's got it."

"I'd like ter look at it again," he said. "I told Mum

to take it away 'cos it kind of fretted me to see that sheep stuck on the rocks and wondering whether maybe the Shepherd couldn't reach it; but seein' as 'ow it's Jesus, I specs He could reach anywhere, couldn't He?"

"Oh, yes," I answered, with perfect confidence, "Jesus can reach anywhere; nobody could go away so far that Jesus couldn't bring them back. Mr. Robinson told me so, so you needn't worry about the sheep. It's all right."

"What I'd like," went on Terry rather dreamily, "would be a picture of that there sheep after the Shepherd had took him up—when he was safe like, in the Shepherd's arms and being carried home; I'd like that fine."

"Would you, Terry?" I inquired eagerly. "I'll try to get you one. I'll look everywhere and see what I can find."

Terry gave a wan little smile and seemed too tired to talk any more; so we sat in silence until his mother came up to settle him for the night. I slipped downstairs to see whether Philip had finished his lessons.

Chapter 22

CARRIED HOME

I DID NOT FORGET my resolve, and on the first Saturday of the autumn term I set out to ask Mr. Robinson's advice about the picture. Philip had stayed at school to play in a football match, so I had to go alone.

I did not mind much, though, because I loved the walk to Mr. Robinson's parsonage, and this Saturday was a clear, windy day full of the scents of wet autumn leaves and bonfires. The woods stretched away in golds and russets, and the hedges gleamed with cuckoopint berries shining like fairy lamps in the dark undergrowth. Here and there I stopped to fill my pockets with chestnuts and smooth pink and green acorns. I felt happy and alive, and when a nearby robin puffed out his breast and sang an early winter song I wished I could join in; I picked a wreath of berries and wound it round my hair and imagined myself a woodland fairy, although I am sure I did not look in the least like one,

213

with my straight, dark braids and my plain, freckled face.

Mrs. Robinson was sitting at the window sewing, so I stopped and had a chat and a chocolate cookie with her. The twins were rolling about in their pen, and I couldn't leave without a game with them—so by the time I eventually reached the church where Mr. Robinson was arranging for the Sunday services the afternoon was passing, and I felt that I must waste no time in unnecessary explanations.

"Mr. Robinson," I started, walking up the aisle very fast, "do you remember that picture you gave me?"

He stopped what he was doing and sat down on the steps; I sat down beside him. It was a rather nice thing about Mr. Robinson—he always gave you his whole attention.

"Indeed, I remember it very well," he replied. "Because, as you know, I have the same one hanging in my room."

"Oh, yes," I answered, "of course you have. But, Mr. Robinson, I want to get the next picture to that one. Do you think it would be possible? Do you think there *is* such a picture?"

Mr. Robinson looked very puzzled.

"I'm afraid I don't understand what you mean by the

next picture," he said, gently. "Do you mean another picture by the same artist?"

"Oh, no," I answered. "I don't mind who's painted it—I mean a picture of what happens next, after the Shepherd has picked up the sheep, and when it's safe in His arms. You see, Terry doesn't like my picture. It makes him feel unhappy because he says he can never feel sure when he looks at it that the Shepherd will really be able to save that sheep. You see, the Shepherd's arms don't look very long and the sheep is a long way down the precipice, and sometimes it bothers Terry, so I thought I'd try and get him the next picture, where the sheep is safe, and where there's nothing more to bother about."

Mr. Robinson's eyes had never left looking at me, and when he answered his voice was very earnest.

"I will try my very hardest to get Terry the next picture," he said. "But, Ruth, you mustn't let Terry think that about the sheep. Do you think you could teach him a text, if I taught it to you first?"

"Oh, yes," I answered, "I'm sure I could. I've taught him lots already. Is it a Shepherd text?"

"Not exactly," said Mr. Robinson. "At least, it doesn't actually mention the Shepherd, but it's about Him all the same. It's this: 'He is able to save to the uttermost.' Do you know what 'the uttermost' means, Ruth?"

I didn't.

"It means as far as anybody could go. It means that however far the sheep had strayed, however high it had climbed, however low it had fallen, the Shepherd could still reach it. It means that there are no people in the world, however naughty or however far away from God, whom the Lord Jesus cannot save as soon as they ask Him."

I looked up quite satisfied. "To the uttermost," I repeated carefully. "Yes, I'll remember that and tell Terry, and then he needn't worry about that sheep any longer. Thank you, Mr. Robinson."

"And on Monday," my friend promised, as we left the church hand in hand, "I am going over to Hereford and I will see if I can find in the shops the picture you want."

I told Terry all about the new text and we said it over together that night; he was glad to learn it, and promised to feel quite certain about the poor sheep getting safe home, because "to the uttermost" meant that even the worst precipices couldn't stop the Shepherd finding that sheep.

But poor Terry was very tired that night—so tired that I stayed with him only a few minutes. His face looked even whiter than usual, and he kept screwing it up as though the pain were very bad. His mother had hardly left him all day, and my aunt had been cooking wonderful little dishes to try to tempt his appetite, but it was all no good. Terry turned his face to the window and lay silent and uninterested.

Several days passed and the beech leaves outside began to fall rapidly; Terry seldom spoke, but he liked watching them whirling about. Although his mother sat beside him most of the time, he usually lay looking out. The doctor came two or three times during the week, but each time he looked so sad that I dared not ask him how Terry was getting on, and when he would be able to play again.

It was one afternoon about tea-time that I came bounding in from school to find that Philip was late. So, flinging down my satchel, I clattered upstairs and then stopped short at Terry's door and opened it softly, for during the past few days even I had come to realize that I ought to be quiet.

But I stopped in amazement at the threshold, for beside the bed sat Mr. Robinson, and Terry's drawn face was turned toward him with something like a smile on it, while he listened to a story about a tiger.

I drew up a stool and listened, too, until the tiger was dead and buried under a palm tree; then Mr.

Robinson drew a flat parcel from under his coat. "We waited till you came to open this, Ruth," he said.

With eager hands I tore off the paper and string while Terry watched, and when it was unwrapped and the picture lay before us we were so pleased that we did not say anything at all; we both just gave a little gasp and sat staring at it.

It was a framed picture of a meadow full of clean white sheep all walking one way and nibbling the grass as they went. In front of them walked a Shepherd with a crook, and in His arms lay a little lamb peacefully asleep.

It was Terry who broke the silence.

"Where's 'e carryin' 'im to?" he asked suddenly, in his fretful voice.

"Home, Terry," answered Mr. Robinson, with a look on his face that I did not then understand. "Safely through each day until they get home."

"Where's home?" went on Terry.

"It's the place where the Shepherd lives and where we see Him face to face," Mr. Robinson replied. "Shall I read you something about Home, Terry?"

The boy nodded, and Mr. Robinson took his New Testament out of his pocket and read in his slow, clear voice about a city where God lived.

"And God shall wipe away all tears from their eyes;

and there shall be no more death, neither sorrow nor crying, neither shall there be any more pain."

There was another long silence, broken again by Terry.

"So!" he whispered thoughtfully. "No more pain!" Then, after a minute's thought, he added,

"May everyone go, or only the good'uns?"

"Why, yes," answered Mr. Robinson. "The gate is open for everyone who wishes to go in, and who belongs to the Good Shepherd, whether he's been good or bad. You see, the Good Shepherd died to make every one of us fit to go in. Do you remember the hymn? I'll say it, in case you've forgotten:

> He died that we might be forgiven,
>   He died to make us good,
> That we might go at last to heaven,
>   Saved by His precious blood.
>
> There was no other good enough
>   To pay the price of sin,
> He only could unlock the gate
>   Of heaven, and let us in.

Another silence, and then Terry whispered, "Tell me some more about them tigers."

And while he lay listening to the tiger story, Terry
fell asleep with his hand on his picture, and Mr. Robinson and I tiptoed out of the room.

Philip and I made a shopping expedition the following Saturday; we bought two daffodil bulbs for Terry,
and something to plant them in. We thought we would
put them on the window sill so that he could watch the
green shoots and the golden flower blossoms next
spring. We sat on the floor burying them in the pots,
and Terry lay watching us listlessly.

"Funny," said Philip suddenly. "You wouldn't think
there was a daffodil hidden down inside this dead-
looking old thing, would you?"

"No," I replied, "you wouldn't; there hardly seems
room to pack it all inside; I'm going to bury mine near
the top, and then it will come up quicker."

"It won't make any difference," said Philip. "It won't
come until its proper time, and when that comes, however far under the earth it's lying, it will shoot up at
once."

I was about to argue, when I caught sight of Terry's
face. It was even whiter than usual and all twisted up
with pain. I wriggled nearer the bed and took hold of
his hand.

"Oh, poor Terry!" I cried. "Is it very, very bad?
Shall I fetch your mother?"

He shook his head.

"No," he whispered. "She takes on so when the pain's real bad." Then with a little sob, he added. "Wish I could go to that place where there ain't no more pain."

Philip and I were dreadfully upset, for we had never seen Terry like this before; he was a wonderfully brave little boy and hardly ever mentioned his sufferings.

"I think," said Philip softly, after an uneasy silence, "that we'll ask God to take away your pain and help you go to sleep—like in the Gospels when people came to Him and He stopped their pains. Kneel down, Ruth, and let's try."

Philip had never prayed out loud before, and the words came very haltingly.

"Dear God—please take away Terry's pain—please make him well soon—please let him go to sleep— Amen."

Then we opened our eyes and looked hopefully at Terry, for we almost expected to see the shadow of pain pass at once. Terry's eyes were open already and fixed on his picture which hung just above his bed.

There were many footsteps up and down in the house that night while we lay asleep, for my aunt and Terry's mother did not go to bed at all, and the doctor arrived just before midnight. No one heard the feet of the Good Shepherd when He drew near and picked Terry up in His arms.

So Philip's prayer was answered in a way we had never dreamed. Before the sun had risen again, while the stars were still high in the sky, Terry had left his twisted, suffering body, and all his pain behind him forever. The Shepherd had carried him Home.

Chapter 23

MR. TANDY EXPLAINS

THE PATH TO THE WOOD was almost overgrown with yellow fern and completely arched by golden beeches, but I pressed on because I wanted to get right into the heart of it, far away from everybody, where I could sit and think about the strange things that had happened since Terry died.

When they told me next morning that Terry had gone in the night I had wept bitterly, because I loved Terry—but I had not felt afraid. Fear came later, when I had thrown myself down on Terry's grave and refused to leave it until my aunt had had to pull me by the hand to make me come home.

Everyone else had gone away, even his mother, and the October mists were falling and the light was growing dim; but I could not bear to leave Terry lying alone in the earth, where I had seen him laid in the early afternoon when the sun was shining.

"Poor little Terry! How cold and lonely he will be!"
I had said to myself over and over again, as I lay in bed
crying bitterly, and even Philip could not comfort me.
In the end I had sobbed myself to sleep and, tired out
by the strain of the day, I slept long and deeply.

My aunt came to awaken me next morning, but
when she saw my pale face and my damp, tangled hair,
she slipped away and left me. Philip got up and went
off to school. Uncle Peter went off to business, and my
aunt set about her daily work; the sun climbed the sky,
but still I slept. When I finally awoke it was dinnertime
and I leaped out of bed in amazement because the sun
had traveled right up the sky and was shining on the
back garden.

Dinner was a silent meal. When it was over I set off
for a walk in the woods; my aunt came to the gate with
me, and kissed me good-by and gave me toffee candy,
which was comforting. I still felt very unhappy as I
crossed the wet fields, where the cows grazed, and the
toadstools grew in fairy rings at my feet.

I walked a long way, because I was not thinking
where I was going; I just wandered, kicking at the
damp leaves and brushing aside the yellow fern and
trying to forget that we had left Terry in the earth. But
I could not forget; and when at last I came to a clearing
where a great chestnut tree spread out its branches, I

lay down on the roots, and resting my head against the trunk, my tears fell thick and fast on the moss.

I was so tired and so miserable that I never heard slow, heavy steps rustling through the leaves, and I quite jumped when a well-known voice above me spoke to me.

"Why, little maid, little maid," said the voice, "what be all this about? Ye'll catch your death of cold lying there on the ground."

It was Mr. Tandy. He stooped down and wrapped his big rough coat about me just as though I had been one of his own stray lambs. Then he sat down on the root, and I snuggled up against him in the big coat and gave a very big sniff.

I had not seen Mr. Tandy for several months because he had left our district to go and work at the Cradley sheepfolds. I was very pleased, but very surprised to see him, and for a moment I wondered whether Mr. Tandy always turned up when anything small was lost and frightened. Then I decided that of course he couldn't have known that I should be there, and looking up at him I asked him what he was doing.

He had come into the wood to cut stakes to mend a gap in the fold, and he carried an axe in his hand. But he laid it down beside him and asked me again what I was crying about.

Very glad to have someone to talk to after my lonely walk, I told my old friend my whole story all about Terry and his pain, and his picture, and how he had come to live with us and hadn't gotten better.

"I prayed so hard he would get better," I said despondently, "but it didn't do any good. God didn't listen, and Terry died."

"Little girl," replied Mr. Tandy rather hesitatingly, "if you come to me and says, 'There's a little lame lamb down yonder what can't run about'—on account of the pasture being steep like, and the stones sharp—and s'posin' I comed down and picked up that there little lamb and carried him in my arms to another pasture where the grass was sweet and the ground easy-like, you wouldn't come and tell me as I hadn't heeded you, would you now?"

I gazed at him dumbly; I was beginning to understand.

"Little girl," he went on, "the Shepherd took His lamb Home, that's all. Ye've no cause to fret."

"But," I cried, my eyes once more filling with tears, "it didn't seem like that at all. They buried Terry in the earth and we left him there, and it seemed so sad and lonely. How can Terry be with the Shepherd when we left him in the earth?"

The old man did not answer for a moment, and then

he started scraping about with his hands among the
leaves as though he were looking for something. His
search was rewarded and he held out a shiny brown
chestnut in one hand, and an empty seed box in the
other—a withered old thing with green prickles turning brown.

"Now tell me," he said, in his slow, thoughtful
voice, "what's a-goin' to happen to the chestnut, and
what's a-goin' to happen to the covering?"

"Oh," I answered, "the case will get buried in the
leaves and then I suppose it will just wither away. It
isn't needed any more; but the chestnut will grow roots
and leaves and turn into a chestnut tree."

"That's right," said Mr. Tandy, encouragingly. "Ye
couldn't have said it better; now, tell me this, little girl;
when you see the young chestnut tree a-waving its little
new leaves in the sunshine next spring, with the birds
a-singing round it, and the rain a-watering of it, you
ain't goin' to fret any more for that old case what's
crumbled away under the leaves, be you?"

"No-o," I answered, with my eyes fixed on his face.
Once more I thought I understood.

"Well, then," said the old man, triumphantly, "you
cease fretting for what you laid below the
ground—t'weren't nothing but the case. Terry's a-

growing strong in the sunshine up yonder, along by the side of his Saviour."

His kind old eyes lit up with joy as he spoke; he threw down the chestnut and case, shouldered his axe and rose stiffly to his feet, because his knees were "full of rheumatics" as he had once told me. Then he unwrapped me and asked me to go home.

"For if I don't get along," he said, "I shan't get that there gap mended up, and my sheep'll be strayin' out again. Good-by, little maid, and God bless you."

I watched him as he moved off into the golden shadows of the wood, and then I stooped down and picked up the chestnut and its case. Clutching them tightly in my hands, I set off home rather fast, for I was cold and tired and the twilight was falling. When I reached our fields again, the sky was aglow with orange light, and against the sunset stood a little black figure scanning the landscape. It was Philip, and he had come to look for me.

I ran to him and put my hand into his, and we walked along in comfortable silence. As we climbed the stile, he glanced at my other hand.

"What are you holding so tight?" he asked curiously.

I unlocked my fist and held out my new treasure.

"It's a chestnut and its case," I said shyly, "and it's like Terry—Mr. Tandy told me so."

"Why?" asked Philip.

"Because," I answered, finding it difficult to explain, "what we put in the earth was like the case; it doesn't matter because Terry didn't need it any more. The inside part that's alive has gone with the Shepherd, so I'm not really sad about it now. Mr. Tandy said it was like a lamb being taken to another field where the grass is nicer."

Philip nodded understandingly. "I see," he said, "and I'm glad you're not sad any more."

When we got home, we found that my aunt had lighted a fire in the nursery, and she, Terry's mother, Philip and myself were going to have supper. It was a lovely, picnicky sort of supper with hard-boiled eggs and gingerbread, rosy apples and pears, and hot cocoa. I had been for a long walk and Philip had been playing football, so we were both starving! We wriggled nearer the blaze and rubbed our shoulders together to show how much we were enjoying it. Even Terry's mother smiled faintly.

It was when we had eaten all we possibly could that my aunt, holding out her hands to the blaze, said softly, "Terry's mother and I have been making plans."

"Have you?" we asked, very much interested. "Tell us?"

"Yes," said my aunt, "because it's a plan that you can

both help in—in fact, I shall need your help a great deal. You see, now that little Terry has gone, we want to do something in memory of him. Terry was weak and ill, and we couldn't help him get better—but there are other weak, ill children whom perhaps we could help to get better—and now that I have Terry's mother to help me in the house, and Ruth is getting so handy, I was thinking we'd try to find some of these children and have them here in the holidays. I used to know someone who worked in a prison in London, and I think he could help us. I thought I would write to him and ask him to find two or three little children who needed good food and country air, and invite them here for Christmas; we would give them as lovely a time as possible. Would you like it, Philip and Ruth?"

We thought it a wonderful idea, and both began to talk at once, eagerly planning what we would do to make it a happy Christmas for them. It was a great relief, for somehow, since Terry died, we had almost felt as though we ought not to talk about other things, but now we could talk freely and happily about this. It was all because of Terry and somehow part of Terry.

So we planned about Christmas stockings and Christmas carols and Christmas dinners and Christmas trees, and our cheeks got redder and redder in the firelight and our eyes grew brighter and brighter.

"Auntie," I cried at last, cuddling up against her, "it *is* a good idea; how *did* you think of it?"

"Well," replied my aunt, "you are fond of 'Shepherd' texts, so I'll tell you how I thought of it. It was the morning I went to visit Terry for the first time; as I walked through the woods I remembered a verse I had forgotten for years. It is what the Lord Jesus said to one of His disciples just before He went back to heaven. He said, 'Feed My lambs'—and that's why I wanted Terry to come to us so badly. Then when he died, three mornings ago, I said to myself, 'This lamb doesn't need me any more; but there are plenty of others . . .' "

She stopped and stared into the fire. I held my hands out to the blaze, and we all sat thinking our own thoughts—sad thoughts about Terry, but all mixed up with happy thoughts about Christmas and the future.

The telephone bell startled us, and my aunt went to answer it. She was gone some time, and when she returned she was laughing, and her face looked most mysterious.

"Another piece of news," she announced, "and this is the very nicest piece of news we've had for years."

We both stared at her in astonishment. Then suddenly Philip jumped to his feet and made a dash at her.

"I know!" he shouted, "I can guess! Mommy and Daddy are coming home!"

Auntie nodded. "Yes," she answered, "you've guessed right. They will be here in time for Christmas."

Philip's face, flushed with the firelight, was radiant with joy; but I stayed perfectly still with my hands clasped on my knees. I suddenly felt miserable and obstinate, and all my old fears came back to me; I remembered Aunt Margaret's words of long ago, and how she had said that I should be such a disappointment to my mother, and I didn't want to meet her. She would like Philip better and I would be cross and unhappy and jealous again—and things were just beginning to get comfortable. I turned my head away and looked gloomily at the coal bucket.

Philip gave me an impatient little shake.

"Aren't you pleased?" he almost screamed. "Why don't you say so?"

I gave a little shrug of my shoulders.

"Yes," I replied, because that was what everyone expected me to say. Then I got up, because I wanted to get away from them. "It's bedtime," I said, coldly. "Good night, Aunt Margaret."

But it wasn't really Good night, for half-an-hour later Aunt Margaret came softly to where I lay in the dark, and knelt by my bed.

"Ruth," she whispered, and her voice sounded all troubled, "why aren't you glad, like Philip?"

I wriggled uncomfortably and buried my hot face in the pillows; but my aunt did not go away; she waited patiently. Seeing that she really expected an answer, I whispered back.

"You said she wouldn't like me, and I don't suppose she will."

"Oh, Ruth!" cried my aunt, "I never said that; I said she would be disappointed when you behaved rudely and selfishly, but that was a long time ago. I know you have been trying hard to be good, and something has certainly made a difference to you. I have felt much happier about you lately, and of course your mother will love you dearly."

I stopped wriggling and lay quite still. I had suddenly stopped feeling shy.

"I know what it is," I answered quietly. "It's my picture; it's knowing the Shepherd that's made the difference."

"Yes," agreed my aunt, "you're right. Your picture, and learning about the Shepherd, has made a tremendous difference to all of us."

Chapter 24

A PERFECT CHRISTMAS

It was christmas evening. We had had such a happy day that I kept having to stop and tell myself that it was all really true.

Mother and Father had arrived just two weeks before, and Philip and I had missed school and gone to Liverpool with Uncle Peter to meet the boat that brought them. We had been on a moving staircase, and we had stayed in a hotel where we had chicken and ice cream, and we had gone up to bed in an elevator and the elevator man had let Philip work it. Then we had been awakened early, and gone down to the Merseyside in a wet, windy dawn; we had watched the passengers streaming down the gangway of the great ocean liner, until Uncle Peter had suddenly said, in a quiet voice, "Here they come." There were Mother and Father showing their passports.

Philip, absolutely trustful and joyful, had flung him-

self straight into Father's arms, and had then turned to
Mother and hugged the hat right off her head! But I
stood still, because I wanted to be quite sure of everything first. When Mother ran toward me I looked up
into her face and suddenly knew that I had found what
I'd been wanting all these years without knowing it. I
was so overcome with this discovery that I just went on
staring up at her, and she didn't hurry me. She waited,
looking down at me, until I was ready and held up my
arms to kiss her. Then she stooped and drew me to her,
and there on the loading bank, with the rain falling,
and the crowds jostling, and the fog-horns wailing, she
told me in a whisper how much she loved me, and I
made up my mind, then and there, that I was never
going to be parted from her again.

With one hand in Mother's and one in Father's, and
with Philip prancing around us like an excited puppy,
we made our way back to the hotel, had kippered
herring and toast and marmalade for breakfast, and
nearly missed the train home.

We were going to live at Aunt Margaret's house
until we could find a home of our own, so we were all
there to welcome three white-faced little Londoner
children who arrived a week later. At first they seemed
ill at ease, and scared of having to sleep alone in a bed,
and they didn't seem to like ordinary food, either. We

put them all three in a double bed and gave them fish and chips for supper, and after that they cheered up and began to enjoy themselves.

The first morning we had all gone out with Father to find a little Christmas tree in the woods. We planted it in a pot when we got home, and wrapped the pot in red, crinkly paper; we were only just in time, too, for that night the snow fell and all the little Christmas trees in the wood were buried.

The little Londoners had never seen white snow before—only gray sooty slush—and they were wildly excited. After breakfast we dressed Alfie and Libby in overcoats much too big for them, and we all set out across the field to take Mr. Tandy a pair of woolly mittens which I had been knitting for weeks. Little Minnie stayed in the kitchen with Terry's mother, whom she adored. In fact, during her three weeks' stay she seldom left her side, and what with all the scrappings and pickings and tastings and tidbits, little Minnie got so fat that she had to go back to London in one of my dresses.

The fields lay in white unbroken stretches, and the sky behind the hills was powder blue. Everything sparkled, and a fat robin sat on the hedge and trilled for Christmas. We reached Mr. Tandy's shack, warm and

breathless, and Mr. Tandy's rosy-faced Mrs. Tandy
opened the door and welcomed us.

We gathered around a blazing log fire, drank hot
cocoa, and made friends with a sick sheep who was
lying near the fireplace on a sack. Mr. Tandy was out in
the woods cutting stakes.

The day before Christmas we took to the road again,
in the clear frosty sunshine, to carry Christmas presents
to the Robinsons. I had made little woolly balls for the
twins and Philip had made a calendar out of his favor-
ite woodpecker postal card for Mr. and Mrs. Robinson,
so we felt we really had something worth taking. We
slid wildly and threw snowballs at each other all the
way, and when we got to the parsonage we decided to
go to the back door and pretend to be carol singers. We
sang "Away in a Manger," because it was the only carol
that Alfie and Libby knew by heart, and Mrs. Robinson
was surprised and came to the door with a twin under
each arm to give us a penny.

How we all laughed, and how pleased Mrs. Robinson was to see Alfie and Libby! We kicked the snow
from our boots, and crowded into the nursery where
Mrs. Robinson served mincepies and a hot ginger
drink, and we gave the twins their balls at once, because I wanted to see whether they liked them or not.
Of course they shouldn't really have had them till

Christmas, but, as Mrs. Robinson said, their memories were very bad at that age, and if they had them again in their stockings they would not remember that they had ever seen them before. The twins, being at a toddling stage, rushed into opposite corners with them and began eating them at once. Mrs. Robinson said that was just because they weren't used to woolly balls.

It was on the way home that Philip had the good idea of learning a carol to sing to Mother and Father and Auntie and Uncle on Christmas Day. He was in the Junior choir at school, and they had learned a new one which he offered to teach us then and there. So he taught us, verse by verse, as we kicked our way along through the soft powdery snow.

And then it was Christmas evening and the great moment of the day was approaching. We had opened our stockings, and been to church, and eaten turkey and Christmas pudding until we all felt as tight as drums. We had been for a walk on the hills in the afternoon with Father and Uncle Peter, and we had come back as hungry as though the dinner had all been a dream. We had had tea by rosy candlelight. Father cut the cake with his Indian dagger and we all burst colorful balloons; but little Minnie didn't like the noise and had been carried out screaming, and fed with chocolate cookies in the kitchen by Terry's mother. Now Auntie

was saying, "Run away for five minutes, children," and
Mother was saying, "Go into the kitchen and see how
Minnie is getting on," and Father was saying, "Anyone
who comes into the drawing room will be eaten by a
big brown bear," and Philip was pinching us all in
turns and saying, "Come on, everybody, now's our
chance."

So when the drawing room door was safely shut on
the grown-ups, we slipped on our coats and tiptoed out
of the front door. The world was quite silent and the
starlight lay silvery on the snow. Philip looked at us
intently and hummed the note, and then we all threw
back our heads and started singing:

> The shepherds had an angel,
>   The wise men had a star,
> But what have I, a little child,
>   To guide me home from far,
> Where glad stars sing together
>   And singing angels are?

How lonely it was! I imagined some small, lost
child, thin and crying, like little Minnie alone in the
snow on a dark, starless night. Still, it all came right in
the next verse; I sang a little louder to reassure myself:

> Lord Jesus is my Shepherd,
>   And I can nothing lack.
> The lambs lie in His bosom
>   Along life's dangerous track.
> The willful lambs that go astray
>   He bleeding fetches back.

I remembered my picture, and the precipice, and the rocks, and the Shepherd with the bleeding hands: of course it was all right. The child in the snow would be found and carried home just like the lamb on the precipice.

> Lord Jesus is my guiding star,
>   My beacon light in heaven.
> He leads me step by step along
>   The path of life uneven;
> He, true Light, leads me to that land
>   Whose days shall be as seven.

I flung my head back and looked at the frosty, jeweled sky and the misty cloud of the Milky Way straggling across it. The stars looked millions of miles away, but that Land was somewhere beyond them—and Terry was there. He had been led to that land and perhaps now he was singing Christmas carols with the angels just as it said in the next verse:

> Those shepherds through the lonely night
>   Sat watching by their sheep,
> Until they heard the heavenly host
>   Who neither tire nor sleep,
> All singing Glory, Glory,
>   In festival they keep.

My thoughts flew back to the shepherds stealing down through the snow and finding the Baby Jesus asleep in the manger. I remembered the Robinson twins, tucked in cradles, with their downy heads burrowed into white pillows, and my heart felt sad for the little sleeping Saviour; I longed to pick Him up and shelter Him, and keep Him warm and safe.

But we had reached the last verse, and were singing our loudest, Philip's clear, bell-like voice soaring high above the rest of us:

> Christ watches me, His little lamb,
>   Cares for me day and night,
> That I might be His own in heaven;
>   And angels clad in white
> Shall sing their Glory, Glory,
>   For my sake in the height.

So it was all right again after all; He wasn't a helpless little Baby any longer, He was the Shepherd Jesus who was going to look after me day and night and carry me Home some day to where Terry was. I looked out into the wide white world with its snow, and smiled—I knew that I was perfectly safe for ever and ever.

But the carol was over and Alfie was hammering excitedly on the door. It was flung open, and there in the hall, under the mistletoe and holly, were Mother and Auntie in paper caps, and Father and Uncle pretending they didn't know it was us, and Terry's mother with tears in her eyes and little Minnie clasped tightly in her arms. We flung ourselves wildly upon them.

"Did you like it?" we shouted. "Did you really think it wasn't us?"

But at that moment a piercing shriek from Libby made everybody jump. She had caught sight of something through the open drawing room door and was making for it. With one accord we fled up the hall behind her and crowded in. The candles on the beautifully decked Christmas tree were lighted and shedding a rosy glow over the dark room.

It was so pretty that we stopped screaming, and sat down quietly, cross-legged on the floor. Alfie and Libby opened their eyes so wide that I could see all the candles reflected in them, and when Father started giving

out the presents their thin bodies trembled with joyful
excitement.

There was a beautiful doll for Minnie, with a yellow
curly wig and clothes that came off. She took it in her
arms and kissed it, and then cuddled down on Terry's
mother's lap, and resting her cheek against the flaxen
wig took no more interest in anything.

Libby had a little bright green dress made by Aunt
Margaret, and a jump-rope with blue and orange han-
dles. We dressed her up at once and led her in triumph
to the long mirror in the hall, where she stood gazing
at herself, her eyes aglow and her thin white cheeks
scarlet with pleasure. I thought she suddenly looked
quite beautiful, and so did Alfie, for he slapped her on
the back and cried out, "Libby! yer don't half look a
stunner!" whereupon everybody laughed, and we all
went back to the Christmas tree.

But Alfie forgot all about Libby when he got his
present. How Aunt Margaret knew that Alfie had been
praying for a pair of roller-skates for nearly a year we
never discovered, but someone must have told her, for
there they were, silver and shining and just the right
size. Alfie didn't say much, but his grunts meant a good
deal, and when Aunt Margaret took a last look at him
that night she found him lying asleep with the roller
skates clasped in his arms.

Philip and I had been taking a real interest in the little Londoners' presents, but now our interest suddenly became personal, for it was our turn. Father took a square parcel from the pile at the bottom of the tree, and handed it to Philip.

"Open it carefully, Phil!" he warned. "It's very fragile."

Philip annoyed me by taking a long time over the unwrapping. He always liked to spin out his pleasures as long as possible. However, at last it came to light, and Philip made a funny noise in his throat like something trying not to explode. It was a Kodak just like the one we had so often gazed at in the shop.

"Philip!" I squealed. "You've got it!" Then I stopped short, for of course it was my turn now. Father had selected a flat, hard parcel and was holding it out to me.

Everyone crowded around to watch as I, unlike Philip, tore the wrappings off as quickly as possible and gave a little gasp of delight and went pink all over.

It was my own picture, but not a crumpled, torn, postal card one. It was a big, beautiful copy in a carved wooden frame for me to hang over my bed and keep. In fact, it was just like the one in Mr. Robinson's study.

The grown-ups opened their presents after that, and they seemed as pleased as we were. They were mostly

home-made things and we were very proud of them:
book-ends for Uncle Peter, a purse for Aunt Margaret,
a blotter for Father and a hot-water bottle cover for
Mother; Terry's mother was presented with a highly-
colored embroidered hanky sachet, which she admired
very much indeed.

Of course, there were other presents, too, but these
were the main ones; and by the time everyone had
opened everything Minnie was found to be fast asleep
in Terry's mother's arms and Libby in her green dress
was nodding against the wall. So they were carried off
and tucked in, and Alfie went up, too, as they didn't
want him waking his little sisters later.

So Philip and I helped clear up, and then Philip and
Father sat down on the sofa together and looked at the
bird book together for about the tenth time. But it was
different now, because the camera lay in Philip's lap
and they were planning the photos.

I wandered off with my picture in my arms, and
climbed the stairs. I wanted to curl up behind the
curtain on the landing window-sill and look out at the
Christmas stars and snow, and listen to the bells that
were ringing from the nearby church. When I reached
my hiding place, I found that Mother had gotten there
first, and that was even better than being alone, so I

climbed on her lap and held up my picture, because I
wanted us to look at it together.

"Isn't it beautiful?" I asked.

"Yes," replied my mother, "but what made you love
it so specially, Ruth? Tell me."

So I told her, rather shyly, and she listened, looking
out over the snow, until I had finished.

"And it's not only me," I ended; "He found me first,
but after that He found Philip and Terry's mother, and
He found Terry, too, and carried him right Home; and,
Mommy, sometimes I think perhaps He found Aunt
Margaret, too. At least, I think she had forgotten about
Him a bit, and when she saw the picture it reminded
her of Him again."

"Yes, I think it did," answered Mother, "and do you
know, Ruth, I also want to learn so much more about
Him; won't it be lovely all learning together? Sometimes, far away in India, I used to kneel down and pray
that you would come to know Him."

I looked up quickly.

"Did you really?" I exclaimed. "Then I suppose
that's why it all happened. I suppose you sort of sent
Him to us. I'm glad it's like that, because it makes it
even nicer than it was before."

I laid my head against her shoulder, and we sat
looking out. I think I nearly fell asleep, and in a dream-

ing sort of way I saw us all sought and found, and following through the green fields in Terry's picture: Mother and Father, Auntie and Uncle; Mr. and Mrs. Robinson and the twins, their tiny feet stumbling through the daisies; old Mr. Tandy with his flock behind him; Terry's mother; Philip and me; Alfie and Libby and Minnie—because I had promised to tell them all about my picture in the morning—and, in front of us all, the Good Shepherd with the wounded hands leading us on to a beautiful Home far away, where Terry was, strong and perfectly happy.

THE END

Moody Press, a ministry of the Moody Bible Institute, is designed for education, evangelization and edification. If we may assist you in knowing more about Christ and the Christian life, please write us without obligation to: Moody Press, c/o MLM, Chicago, Illinois 60610.